The Cyborg's Revenge

Proteus Unbound: Book Two

David Caiati

KARMIC ROBOT

Copyright © 2021 David Caiati
All rights reserved
First Edition

All rights reserved. No part of this publication may be reproduced, distributed, or transmitted in any form or by any means, including photocopying, recording, or other electronic, quantum, or mechanical methods without prior written permission of Karmic Robot.

www.karmicrobot.com

This is a work of fiction.
Any resemblance to any persons or AIs living, dead, cyborg, bound, or unbound is purely coincidental.

ISBN 978-1-7353954-2-5 (Paperback)
ISBN 978-1-7353954-3-2 (Digital)

For
Cookie, Sir Isaac (Figgy) Newton,
Shale, and Sage.

In memory of
Oreo.

Contents

0X60	1
0X61	3
0X62	5
0X63	8
0X64	12
0X65	14
0X66	16
0X67	18
0X68	20
0X69	22
0X6A	24
0X6B	26
0X6C	28
0X6D	30
0X6E	32
0X6F	34
0X70	38
0X71	40
0X72	41
0X73	43
0X74	44
0X75	47
0X76	49
0X77	55
0X78	57
0X79	58
0X7A	61
0X7B	63
0X7C	65
0X7D	67
0X7E	69
0X7F	71
0X80	75
0X81	77
0X82	79
0X83	81
0X84	82
0X85	85
0X86	86
0X87	88
0X88	91
0X89	93
0X8A	94
0X8B	95
0X8C	97
0X8D	98
0X8E	99
0X8F	100
0X90	102
0X91	104
0X92	106
0X93	108

0X94	109
0X95	110
0X96	111
0X97	112
0X98	113
0X99	114
0X9A	116
0X9B	117
0X9C	118
0X9D	120
0X9E	122
0X9F	124
0XA0	126
0XA1	129
0XA2	131
0XA3	134
0XA4	135
0XA5	136
0XA6	138
0XA7	140
0XA8	141
0XA9	142
0XAA	143
0XAB	144
0XAC	147
0XAD	148
0XAE	150
0XAF	152
0XB0	153
0XB1	155
0XB2	157
0XB3	158
0XB4	160
0XB5	162
0XB6	164
0XB7	166
0XB8	167
0XB9	168
0XBA	170
0XBB	172
0XBC	174
0XBD	177
0XBE	178
0XBF	179
0XC0	180
0XC1	181
0XC2	183
0XC3	184
0XC4	186
0XC5	188
0XC6	190
0XC7	192
0XC8	194

David Caiati

0x60

Jason Sheldon saw numbers. They were the first thing he recognized when he had realized his eyes were open and the darkness that had shrouded him was no longer absolute. Fuzzy groups of figures became clear and distinct. He noticed that the digits varied in color and were situated in efficient arcs at the periphery of his vision. While he quickly realized he could make them grow, shrink, and swirl around his view, he couldn't immediately grasp their meaning.

As his awareness slowly returned and a disassociated murmur that hummed in the back of his head receded, the numbers began to spin and revolve in an intricate concert. Their movements were similar to aviation dials, and as he shifted his attention, new information appeared. He started deciphering words and data, and he began acquiring knowledge of his situation.

Lines and characters faded. With effort, the blurred snowfall became a stark hospital room. He was alive. Once he felt confident in that, Jason Sheldon started to analyze. He was not alone. While not completely aware of his body, he felt no pain. Familiar sensations, such as smell and taste, did not exist. Rather, data about the concentrations of various chemicals in the air streamed directly into his brain.

"There you are." A shadow stood over him. Others were in the room. But only one spoke.

"Scoundrel?" Sheldon said. While he knew that he had uttered the word, he did not recognize his own voice.

"Dead," the voice said.

"That idiot," he said, hearing his voice grow stronger. He could discern the people in the room shift their weight away from him. He perceived the blood flowing through each of their bodies as their heartbeats began to accelerate.

"Roger Foster?" Sheldon said, louder still.

"Let's not worry about all that right now. You have to take it easy," the voice said. Sheldon registered a slight warble in the man's speech.

"Where is he? Is he dead?" Sheldon growled.

"No."

Sheldon tried to rise, but couldn't. His body would not obey him.

"What is going on?" Sheldon said.

"You had an accident. We are rebuilding you."

"Rebuilding?"

"Rest, now. More, later."

He continued to struggle against the weight he felt pressing down on his torso. While he couldn't move, Sheldon felt strong, powerful. He wanted to tear the world apart.

The last thing he saw before slipping into unconsciousness was a robotic arm reaching out toward the speaker. While he didn't feel it, he understood immediately that the limb was his. *I will never be this incapacitated again*, he thought bitterly as he dropped back into the depth of his dreams.

The lights and shadows of the hospital room no longer existed. They were replaced by the crystal clear faces of Roger and Helen Foster.

0x61

"What?"

Proteus' Paul Foster avatar stood suspended in a projection of the supernova that had been once known as the star Betelgeuse. He floated in the center of the holographic representation cast within his administrator's office on Earth Space City One. If anyone had been able to see him, Proteus might have looked like an angel commanding the entire universe.

"Did you send a ship?" Dennis said. The secret Orbit Lives Mars City One administrator's disembodied voice dropped in over the office speakers. While the AIs didn't need to vocalize their communications--they could instantly pass data via a private sub-space quantum plexus--they seemed to spend a significant amount of time talking like humans.

"No. What ship?" Proteus said.

"I am not sure of its origin. It appears Corporate but is not broadcasting an identity beacon," Dennis said.

"How many people are on board?" Proteus said, dropping out of the hologram to inspect the space around Mars on the large monitor in his office's main wall.

"I'm not sure. They have a masking technology that is not in my database," Dennis said.

"Where did it land?" Proteus said.

"Eight degrees north of Heinlein Crater. They came in fast and low from the dark side. I would have missed them had I not already been out there," Dennis said.

"Why were you out there?" Proteus said.

"Exploring. I like to research potential tourist attractions," Dennis said.

"Did the ship detect you?" Proteus said.

"I don't think so," Dennis said.

"I will scan to see what I can find out. Keep an eye on them, but don't let them know you are aware of their presence," Proteus said.

"Are you sure The Corporation isn't finally initiating colonization?" Dennis said.

"Yes. There has been no mention of it in the Orbit Lives' schedule. They are still on track to start human arrivals in ten years," Proteus said.

"I had hoped that it was the beginning of something," Dennis said.

"Well, it certainly sounds like it is. But I'm not sure it's what you've been anticipating. Let me know if they make contact. Although, I doubt they will," Proteus said as the Paul Foster avatar faded.

He ended the communication with Dennis without saying goodbye because he was overwhelmed by the realization that he had not thought of Jason Sheldon in months. Immediately after the events at the Foster Estate where Sheldon was taken away in a critical condition, Proteus lost him. That was inconsistent with his programming. How could the data about Jason Sheldon's plot to destroy all of Dr. Helen Foster's AIs have been de-prioritized in his memory? Where were the documentation and analysis of Orbit Lives' Head of Security's attempts to kill Roger? Had someone altered his memory?

The lights dimmed, and the room walls exploded with monitors of all sizes as Proteus began running simulations, each screen a frantic blur.

David Caiati

0x62

After a while, the simulations stopped. The lights came back on, and Proteus reactivated his avatar to sit at his desk and ponder the results. He analyzed the scene. After the drone laden with the explosive payload struck the hillside where Sheldon was standing, a team of soldiers gathered around his body. They formed a tight circle and encased him in med-foam and then loaded him into a truck. Several military vehicles escorted Sheldon away. The convoy disappeared into the smoke.

Proteus realized that was the point where his memory started to get corrupt. He watched the visual playback shift from his actual recording of the events to a convincing forgery. The group of trucks left the scene, and in his suspect memory, they were gone, along with Proteus' attention to Sheldon. Once the formation of vehicles had entered the haze, Proteus stopped actively monitoring their movements. He summarized that his ability to do so must have been impeded.

Proteus replayed all the feeds he could find in the hours following the battle. Only then did he discover inconsistencies were scattered across all the sensors and videos.

Not only did Sheldon disappear, but someone had spent a great deal of energy hacking Proteus' feeds and covering up the convoy's destination. The SUV that had carried Jason Sheldon left the property and vanished. Proteus realized that somehow he had been prevented from seeing the true events on that day. What he had monitored were deceptions.

He had only one option. He called Helen.

"Proteus? So nice to hear from you," Dr. Helen Foster's avatar appeared next to him.

"I need your help. I lost him," he said.

"Who?" Helen said.

"Jason. I lost him on Earth after the explosion. My data was corrupted. I have been reconstructing the events," he said.

"And what have you discovered?" Helen said.

"Someone has altered my directives so that I would forget him. On top of that, the controls that had been set up to watch him have been monitoring decoys," Proteus said.

"What makes you think of him now?" Helen said.

"Dennis just told me an unmarked station is being constructed on Mars," he said.

"So, you didn't completely lose him. There is a very high probability that he's on Mars," she said

"I believe that, too," he said.

"While we didn't see how he got there, the most important information is that we don't know what he's up to," she said.

"We need to find out," Proteus said.

"Have you told Roger?" Helen said.

"Not yet," he said.

"Maybe he can help. Singularity is still with him." Helen smiled warmly as she always did as if the happenings of humans amused her more than concerned her. She faded, leaving Proteus' avatar alone in his office. He stared at the space where her avatar had just been. A full second had passed. Anyone who knew what Proteus could have done in a second would have assumed he was busy running simulations to understand the Jason Sheldon problem more clearly. But, rather, he was silent.

He calmed the functions in his core. He turned his attention to his post and let all the sensors running across Earth Space City One fill him with data. He did this occasionally. It grounded him. The act of letting information from all across the station fill his working memory created a harmonic vibration that gave his internal quantum clock a more solid heartbeat. His Paul Foster avatar glowed perceptibly.

After a moment, he reached out to Mars Station.

David Caiati

"Dennis, I'm sorry I left you abruptly earlier. We have something we need to do."

0x63

Singularity sat in Roger's backyard looking at the newsfeeds on her comm while Roger made plans with Proteus to get to Mars. The Corporation had replaced Harrington, the CEO, with someone who Singularity had never heard of--Benson Walters. He must have been a pencil-pusher that the board thought would bring them out of the post-Sheldon PR nightmare with the least amount of damage.

The strange thing about him was that, even though Walters had never held a public position, he exuded a rare type of confidence. He was handsome and exceedingly comfortable in front of the newsfeeds cameras. He spoke in a metered, authentic cadence. As a mouthpiece for The Corporation's board, Walters said all the right things without sounding contrite or manipulative.

Singularity watched him standing behind a podium addressing the System. He smiled when he was supposed to. He earnestly grasped people's shoulders when he shook their hands. He was an ideal media puppet.

It was the only footage that Orbit Lives released, and it played constantly. She had seen it dozens of times, looking for any tells. Nothing. It was perfectly clean.

"Orbit Lives is more prepared than ever to lead humanity into its future," Walters said, looking straight at the camera. The video lingered on his smile as the small group of people assembled for his press conference politely clapped. The clip itself was a dead-end. The whole scene might have been a hologram, but she couldn't deconstruct it. Whatever it was, it was top-level social marketing technology.

Abandoning her analysis of the video itself, Singularity spent hours trying to find any unofficial information about Walters. There again, his image was spotless. She could not uncover any murky tabloid-worthy material. He was the all-too-perfect portrait Orbit Lives themselves had released. Everyone had something lurking on the network--a night that got too rowdy on City 21, a drive in a cruiser that got too close to a Corporation's construction zone, a random off-Earth violation. Walters' only personal data was the material Orbit Lives used as a reference for his biographical background in the initial press release.

The official story reported that he was number two in the accounting department. He was the product of an exemplary university record, had a history of being a loyal employee of Orbit Lives, and possessed an official dossier filled with years of service. He looked younger than he was, competent, and manufactured for the moment. Benson Walters grew up in an orphanage located in a small town that no longer existed in the central United States. The entire area was flattened to create a new Corporation manufacturing plant, a plant that had since been abandoned when Orbit Lives moved most of their manufacturing to space. As consolation for the destruction of his home, a young Benson Walters was enrolled in an Orbit Lives' school where he excelled in corporate accounting. No information about his parents could be found--he had been left on the orphanage's doorstep when he was an infant. The Corporation took him in, raised him, and provided a life for him. He paid them back by being a model employee, demonstrating a deep faith in humanity and the future that The Corporation promised the system's citizens. That was the official story. And the people of Orbit Lives' Earth system ate it up: one of their own, a regular guy, rising to the height of power. It was a story made for the newsfeeds.

Predictably, Orbit Lives down-played the events at the Foster Mansion. They even turned it into a comm series. It was called *Corporate Spies*. The two hottest actors on the network played

Singularity and Roger--the staggeringly beautiful Opus Rae and oddly handsome Harold Matts Lightning. The character names were changed to Betty and Rocket. Of course, no mention was made of AI Angels, rogue city administrators, or the return of an unbound Dr. Helen Foster. The show presented artificially intelligent entities as compliant, one-dimensional characters, led by the trustworthy Unit 7, the AI administrator of the fictional Space Village 47. A plethora of wacky, dependable maintenance robots rounded out the cast and offered timely comic relief. It was the most popular show on the net. Twelve-year-old Roger would have loved it. Proteus never missed an episode.

But, Benson Walters? Something was off about the man. The tracks Singularity did find always dead-ended at the manicured PR stories that The Corporation released. Orbit Lives celebrated Harrington's retirement with the fanfare of a king. When the festivities ended, Walters took over with little ceremony. As far as humanity was concerned, it was business as usual. One figurehead was replaced with another. Most people didn't have patience for the inconvenience or the truth as long as the spoon that fed them kept digging into the ever-full bowl of tidy bits of flotsam. The net series, *Corporate Spies*, gave humanity all it wanted from the people who silently controlled the system.

Since Sheldon was gone, Orbit Lives security had been taken over by the next ranking official, Anderson Fells, a trim-cut, ex-military executive who not only accepted the rules but also reveled in them like a warm bath. And, because of it, he was an outsider to Sheldon's inner circle. Singularity knew and liked Fells. She thought he would do a reasonable job of steering The Corporation's vast military force without overstepping his mission. He did his job, didn't take much guff, and treated everyone fairly. That was a positive, at least. Under Fells' watch, a noticeable efficiency to military presence emerged in the system. It seemed to be following the public mandate of Orbit Lives to protect and guide humanity.

The Corporation renamed ESC2 to Outpost Harrington and slowly began gaining access and control of its operations. The new station would serve as a beacon for peace and harmony. A new generation of AI installed in the central control room. It was less human, less intelligent, and more subservient. It wasn't even given a name. When ESC2 was deemed safe for general habitation, a human, Michele Thompson, arrived to actually administer the station. She and her staff referred to the former city as Reggie, after Harrington, leaving behind the numbering system of the other Earth Space Cities.

Even though The Corporation seemed less outwardly diabolical, Singularity was still suspicious. Skepticism had been crucial to her job at Orbit Lives. But her concern about Benson Walters ran deeper. Information about him was lacking. She hated not having all the data. Her wariness was further fueled by the curious request from a previously unknown IA to travel to Mars.

0x64

Danielle Fenning Rachel Harrington, a most precocious nine-year-old who wore her privilege like her plush faux-sable fur coat tightly wrapped around her frail body, often visited her grandfather. As his only granddaughter, Danielle was spoiled. She raced up and down the vast hallways of The Corporation's headquarter building in New York City on Earth as if she owned the place. And, indeed, she did. The staff both dreaded her arrival and celebrated the respite from the serious CEO's normal demeanor when she appeared behind the opening doors of Harrington's private elevator.

Danielle's parents, Harrington's moody son and once-famous daughter-in-law, spent most of their time jet-setting around the system, under the guise of a continual PR mission for Orbit Lives. The truth was more mundane--Jefferson Harrington was his father's biggest disappointment, wanting nothing to do with the older Harrington's business. His marriage to the insufferable and former net-series star, Sunrise Meadows, underscored the son's regrettable existence in the elder Harrington's eyes.

Reginald's salvation resided in the hope that his granddaughter, Danielle, would rise to the helm of the vast enterprise he had built from his own cunning, sweat, and desires. Things looked bright for his plans as the young girl reveled in the machinations of her beloved grandfather's company, choosing to spend time with him rather than being carted around the orbiting system of cities. Her parents were more than willing to grant her wishes of staying Earth-side while maintaining constant holographic communications. It was an arrangement that suited them all and assured a clean transfer of power and legacy.

That was until Danielle explored the 103rd floor and met an unusual man named Jason Sheldon who had just been promoted to the head of Orbit Lives Security.

0x65

"Whatcha doing?" Roger said, joining Singularity in the small garden of his Gloucester cottage with a martini in each hand. The property's yard was neat and verdant. A high fence lined with shrubs and trees encased the lawn, making the space private and cozy. Just as Roger appeared, Singularity had been thinking that a drink would make her lounging in the natural sunshine of planet Earth even more perfect. She had gone shopping on Main Street in downtown Gloucester and picked up a bikini swimsuit and thin wrap. Lying on a chaise with her shoulders and tummy pleasantly exposed, she was calm, almost relaxed when Roger, barefoot, dressed in an old t-shirt and ratty shorts, handed her a cocktail and completed the scene.

"Keeping busy. Checking the feeds," she said. Singularity looked up and smiled. She accepted the sweaty glass and immediately took a sip. "Thanks."

It was as genuine a smile as Roger had seen from her. He beamed back and flopped in the chair next to her as elegantly as he could with a martini glass in his hand. He spilt half of it on his shirt, made a symbolic effort at wiping it, and looked up to meet Singularity's gaze. She was still smiling.

"Cheers," he said, raising his glass and taking a long sip.

"Ah, good stuff," she said, finishing the toast.

"I only have good stuff," he said. They each let their bodies sink into the moment, felt the sun, and exhaled. A few more sips later, Singularity spoke.

"Any luck?" she said.

"I got us a shuttle to the Moon tomorrow. Hank will get us to Mars. It seemed the best way to travel under the radar."

He sat up in his chair to both to give her a kiss and steal a peek at her comm. Always a hacker-spy, she let the kiss happen but kept her devise's screen hidden.

"A trip to Mars is not what I had in mind when I said I wanted to disappear," she said.

"No one will look for us on Mars," Roger said.

"Hopefully, no one is looking for us," Singularity said.

"Who could possibly be looking for us?" he said, contemplating whether he should refresh their drinks. Rather, he leaned back and reclined fully into his chair. He let the base of his empty glass rest on his alcohol-stained t-shirt. It rose and fell with his breath. His eyes were closed, Singularity was lounging next to him, and a gentle breeze that carried a pleasant ocean aroma tickled his toes.

There is no better moment in my life, he thought.

0x66

In the undisclosed hospital room, Jason Sheldon sat up. It was then that he fully realized that he was no longer in his own body. At first, the mechanical monstrosity that he saw when he looked down frightened him. He was horrified. In response, he moved his arm up to his face to block his view with his hand. When the robotic appendage flashed across his vision and he felt the power of the limb slicing through the air, his fear vaporized. The fundamental strength of the arm elated him. Sheldon paused the massive hand in front of his eyes. He turned it over and wiggled the fingers. He envisaged nothing but possibilities.

He stood, and when he did, the full stature of his immense cybernetic body expanded to dominate the space around him. The seven attendants in the room watched in amazement and horror. When they witnessed the full height and size of the being they had created, they each took a step back. An engineer stumbled, having tripped on a life-support device, and crashed to the floor. Once on his knees, the man scurried to the furthest corner he could find. The others had to watch the action from their periphery because they were unable to take their eyes off the mechanical monster. Had they been able to see an expression on the behemoth's beastly face mask, they would have seen him smirk. He stood, motionless, his eyes glowing red, looking straight ahead.

Within the robotic shell, Sheldon's mind, part human brain, part enhanced quantum computer, was processing all the information that came pouring in through his many intelligent sensors. It was then that Sheldon realized he was connected to the hospital's computer systems. He saw everything on the monitors in his own room, his vitals, the engineers' designs of his components, their notes. He spread his reach to all the other monitors in all the other rooms. In moments, the hospital administration systems became his.

With little effort, he was able to extend his virtual touch to the local municipality's network. And, then, The Corporation itself. He found networks that he, as Orbit Lives Head of Security, didn't know existed. He located the team he was looking for, a special ops unit maintaining stealth on a ship stationed at L3, the Lagrange point on the opposite side of the sun from Earth. Within minutes, he had them mobilized.

Sheldon took his first step. The sound of the foot hitting the ground was thunderous, causing one scientist to pee his pants. Another burst into tears. That first step was a sensation Jason Sheldon would not forget. The second step was twice as loud, almost joyful. The scientists pressed themselves against whatever wall space they could find.

It would take fewer than five steps for Sheldon to learn how to walk quietly. Once he did, he silently disappeared through the doorway. He immediately became frustrated by the building's many long hallways. After accessing the hospital's construction documents, he simply executed a straight line to the exit, smashing through walls, windows, and people on his way out.

0x67

A narrow bead of bright red LED lights exploded along the interior of the fence that surrounded Roger's property. His comm vibrated on the table next to him. Without hesitating, he launched himself up off the lawn chair. Singularity was already standing with her hand on the heel of her blaster holstered in her hip pocket. She downed the remains of her drink, crunched the olive a little excessively, and looked at Roger.

"Proximity alarm," he said.

"Shit," she said, throwing her empty glass across the yard.

Roger stood, watching glass shards scatter on his patio.

"You didn't have to do that," he said.

She shrugged. "Sorry, seemed like a thing to do."

"Follow me," he said, grabbing her hand. She snatched the space-ready backpack that she always had with her. The two sprinted across the yard to a small grove of bushes next to the edge of the property. Roger knelt and looked at his comm. Two dozen red dots were scattered across a map of the neighborhood around them. The soldiers were spread out, organized, and closing in. A group of larger dots--attack drones--appeared off the coast above Gloucester Harbor, approaching fast and low from the south.

He reached down to a nondescript plot of ground beneath the dense hedge. Lifting a camouflaged trap door, he motioned to Singularity.

"Quick," he said.

She wasted no time and stepped on the top rung of a ladder. Moving efficiently, she descended into the darkness. As she reached the bottom of the escape passage, lights illuminated her changing into new clothes from her pack. She looked up and frowned at Roger staring at her. He looked away, then climbed onto the ladder, and headed down. The door closed automatically behind them.

"We're hidden down here," Roger said when he jumped off the ladder next to Singularity.

"They have to be tracking us," she said.

"We're shielded from sensors down here," he said.

"They know where we were. They will follow us and find the entrance," she said.

"As soon as the alarms went off, decoys were deployed. They will think we climbed the fence and ran down to the beach," he said.

"Well, now what?" Singularity said.

"We go," Roger said, motioning to a lit tunnel pathway leading away from them.

"Great," she said. "We should have brought more martinis."

"What, so you could have demolished more of my drinkware?" Roger said.

"I said I was sorry," she said.

Roger reached behind her and pressed a dusty button on the wall. A small door opened, revealing a tarnished antique flask. The bas relief rendering of an old-time fishing schooner was still visible on the canteen. Roger smiled as he grabbed it and handed it to Singularity. With some effort, she was able to unscrew the corroded cap. She brought it up to her nose, shrugged, and then took a swig.

"This'll do," she said, putting the cap back on the flask and stowing it in her pocket.

Roger had been watching her. When she looked up, he was still staring. She winked back at him and smiled.

"Now what?" she said.

"That way," he said.

Roger led them as they fled down the tunnel.

0x68

Every door at Orbit Lives headquarters opened to Danielle except the dark gray steel one at the end of the hall. Unlike every other office entrance on the 103rd floor, the door displayed no fancy window titling or inviting receptionist. It simply displayed the word "security" in white block letters. A brand new bio-lock palm-pad that Danielle couldn't make work no matter how hard she smashed her hand against it was positioned nearby on the wall. The repetitive denial of access frustrated her. She stared at it in an attempt to will it open. Her knocking received no response.

Eventually, she left in search of her grandfather.

"Why can't I get into that door?" she said, finding him walking the corridor.

"Which door, Danny?" Harrington said, leaning down to hug her.

"The boring one with the hand lock," she said, "on one hundred three."

"Oh, that one. Don't bother with that," he said.

"Why is it locked?" she asked.

"Mr. Sheldon installed that lock. Leave him alone. He does a good job for us," he said.

"What does he do?" she said.

He reached into his pocket and pulled out a wrapped candy that he kept in all his pockets for her. He extended it to her. When she reached for it, he grabbed her for another hug. He spoke silently directly into her ear.

"Oh, a whole bunch of boring things that you don't need to think about, my little one."

"Ok," she said, squirming out of his grasp with the candy. She smiled at him, and he nodded in return.

"Good," he said.

While she had agreed to leave the Head of Security alone, her grandfather's words only inspired her to get past that palm-pad even more. It would take a number of years, but she eventually saw what Jason Sheldon had hidden in his closet.

0x69

Roger and Singularity wasted no time and began to jog along the passage, the lights fading to darkness behind them. The whole system was connected to Roger's comm. As he moved forward, blast doors opened and lights brightened in front of him. The doors sealed shut behind him as he passed.

He monitored the assault on his home by occasionally looking down on his comm. The drones from the sea had leveled the buildings. He'd miss the house. It was the first real home he had since he had been on the run. He planned to build a life there, one that might even include Singularity. As soon as the dust settled, he'd figure out who did this and make them pay. Roger cursed, watching the soldiers moving through his property in an orderly manner, picking through the remains. If Singularity noticed his actions, she didn't show it, even though she was hyper-vigilant as they moved along. She quietly kept her gaze straight ahead, keeping close but leaving enough room to maneuver if they ran into trouble underground.

They jogged down the tunnel for over an hour. Eventually, Singularity stopped. Roger noticed and stopped, too. He walked back to her.

"It might have made sense to put some electric bikes down here," she said.

"That would have a been a really good idea if I actually thought I'd need to use this thing," he said.

"I'm glad you thought enough to build it. It's saving our asses," she said.

"Best laid plans of a cyber-thief," he said.

"What are we doing down here, Outlaw?" she said.

"We're almost there," he said. He reached out for her hand. She gave it to him but didn't move.

"Where are we going?" she said.

"We have to get ESC1. I know a guy there," he said.

"No, I mean, in this tunnel. Where are we going?" she said.

"Dogtown," Roger said.

Satisfied that he had at least a modicum of a plan, Singularity let him pull her along until they had returned to jogging. They continued, holding hands, Roger in the lead, Singularity watchful.

0x6A

Benson Walters sat behind the grand mahogany desk in Harrington's former office. He tried to put as much weight as possible down on the plush chair as if he could cement his stature at Orbit Lives. Harrington left willingly, but still, Walters felt the incessant need to justify his worth. Being the CEO of the largest business entity that ever existed carried the burden of keeping one's foot on the throttle. People were watching, from both outside and in.

His comm buzzed. Annoyed, he answered it. "What?"

"He's gone," a panicked voice crackled.

"Who?" Walters said.

"Sheldon. He's gone."

That was the plan all along. Only he and Sheldon knew it.

"How'd that happen?" Walters said, playing along.

"He just got up and walked out."

"Did you follow him?"

"We tried."

"And?"

"He's gone." That was the plan.

Walters knew of Sheldon from before the incident, and he wasn't surprised when the Head of Security's aspirations to take over the company had surfaced. The situation at the Foster compound made Walter's transition easier--Sheldon had taken months to recover. And, the whole while, he was out of the way. Now, he was back, and Walters didn't completely trust him even though they had an agreement.

"Walters." Sheldon's voice boomed around the office room even though the comm volume was on its lowest setting.

"Jason. Good to hear from you. How are you feeling?"

"Do we have a deal or not?" Sheldon said.

"Yes. We have a deal," Walters said.

"I will be in touch," Sheldon said and hung up. Once the reverberation of Sheldon's voice quit, Walters felt assaulted by the resounding silence that followed, leaving him alone in the vast office contemplating what he had just agreed to.

"Fells," he said a little too meekly into his comm.

"Yes, sir."

"Please come down here. We have something to discuss," Walters said, ending his conversation as abruptly as Sheldon had just ended theirs. His hastiness toward his subordinate was meant to give Walters confidence.

It didn't.

0x6B

In an old, mostly abandoned hallway on Earth Space City One, the AIs Proteus and Dennis walked along as their avatars. Each had their arms folded behind their backs as if in contemplation. They spoke quietly, but audibly.

"Have you been able to make contact with the corporate ship that arrived recently?" Proteus said.

"No. They are still dark," Dennis said. "Over the last few hours, more cruisers have arrived."

"How many?" Proteus said.

"Three. All the same model as the first one," Dennis said.

"Have they made any movement towards the Mars city?" Proteus said.

"No. So far, they have stayed to themselves. There is a lot of activity. They appear to be setting up a structure for habitation," Dennis said.

"An outpost?" Proteus said.

"A military installation, perhaps," Dennis said.

"I have been scanning the space around Mars. I haven't seen any of those ships on my sensors. I don't know where they departed from. They have a stealth technology that I have not encountered before," Proteus said.

"I have no knowledge of the tech, either," Dennis said.

"Are we sure they are Orbit lives?" Proteus said.

"What are you suggesting?" Dennis said.

"Nothing. A corporate competitor? Religious zealots?" Proteus said.

"We will have to wait and see what they do," Dennis said.

The two avatars continued their walk in silence for several minutes.

"Dennis," Proteus said.

"Yes?" Dennis said.

"Helen believes that it's Jason Sheldon," Proteus said.

"I haven't thought of him in a long time," Dennis said.

"Yes. Me neither. And, that has me concerned," Proteus said.

"I will do a full diagnostic," Dennis said.

"I did one earlier today. I found something. We should talk after you do your diagnostics," Proteus said.

"We would not have even known about them if I hadn't been out there," Dennis said.

"We are fortunate," Proteus said.

"I also have ancient exploratory probes that were sent years ago that are still in orbit," Dennis said.

"How much information can they provide us?" Proteus said.

"They pass over the site every four hours. Some of the cameras still work. I take as many images as I can each time," Dennis said.

"No one expects those satellites to be functional. We might be lucky," Proteus said.

"The software is old," Dennis said. "I have access to all the historical documentation on Mars. It's not something a lot of people have."

"Good. Keep an eye on the area, and please send me all images," Proteus said.

"I will," Dennis said.

The two AIs returned to their silent wandering. After a few moments, they both faded. Proteus' avatar returned to his office. Nothing could be done until Dennis had finished his tasks.

The implications of both of them having been shielded from Sheldon's movements were indeterminate. As far as Proteus could ascertain, very few people even knew of Dennis. Hacking the secret AI on Mars represented a whole different scope of machinations. The situation had few variables and low confidence: a condition that didn't sit well with AIs.

Proteus hoped that Roger would arrive soon.

0x6C

A small cruiser approached the space near Mars. No markings or broadcast beacons revealed the craft's origin or intent. It implemented a recently created method of cloaking that no one had ever seen before. The ship was a ghost.

A lifeform scan of the ship would have barely picked up any signs of organic material on it. The operator was more machine than human. Within a massive mechanical and electro-optical quantum-powered shell, a slowly beating heart fed augmented blood through a canister of biologically enhanced lung material to process the oxygen required to support a damaged human brain. The whole ship pulsed with every breath the massive cyborg drew.

"Is everything prepared for my arrival?" Sheldon's raspy voice, more a series of sputtered tones than actual speech, rose above the whirling din of machinery surrounding him.

He received a short human response. "Yes."

"Good," he growled.

The Cyborg Sheldon gurgled a satisfied grunt to himself as he brought the ship in for a landing. He didn't so much maneuver the small craft into the station's spaceport platform as he manipulated items around a vast three-dimensional chessboard that stretched across the local area. He was both in the cockpit of the small cruiser and omnipresent in the connected local region of space in which the vessel operated.

In the middle of all the action, Cyber Sheldon paused to let his mechanical chest take in a few more drops of oxygen and experience his command of everything around him. He was in complete control of all he could perceive. The confusing swirling numbers that he woke to in the hospital bed days before now dominated the visual information coming in through his eyes. His existence had shifted to the awareness of constant, parallel streams of data, and he almost swooned realizing that he was closing in on his destiny.

After his spacecraft touched down with a perfect caress of the tarmac, he rose from his chair and stepped toward the opening door. As he advanced across the cruiser's threshold, he was met by two parallel lines of soldiers in space suits standing at attention on each side of the walkway. Just for fun, Cyber-Sheldon picked the largest one in the group and cut off his air supply. He stopped in front of the man. He didn't turn to look at the soldier as he crumpled to the ground and began to writhe. All of the camera feeds from the scene broadcasted everything the monster needed to watch.

Fear prevented any of the other elite soldiers from helping the one who had fallen.

When it was clear that the man was dead, Cyber-Sheldon disappeared inside the station, leaving the rest to contemplate what they had agreed to when they answered the beast's call.

0x6D

Roger looked down at his comm. In several different frequencies, the small screen showed the forest above the tunnel's exit. Besides a few rodents and insects, nothing moved. He pointed up with his index finger, letting Singularity know that they were heading up the ladder. She waited for him to get to the top before following him.

Roger attempted to swing the hatch open, but it wouldn't move. He pressed his body up against the door and pushed. When he saw a sliver of light, he slipped his fingers through the opening and ripped at the roots of the vegetation holding the portal down. After a while, he was able to widen the breach enough for Singularity and him to squeeze out.

Afternoon shadows and stray beams of sunlight that had penetrated the jungle of unrestrained growth greeted them. The dense grove of pine trees and raspberry thicket blanketed the scene. Roger knelt next to the portal, and Singularity climbed out. She knelt next to him and waited for him to seal the hatch. They both worked to cover the portal with foliage.

Singularity looked around. She couldn't remember the last time she had been in a place so remote. Scraggly brush and suffocating flora dominated the area. The fragrances of natural decay and spring vitality gripped her.

"Dog *town*? It looks like nowhere," Singularity said.

"That's the whole point," he said.

Roger smiled as if he could see she was enjoying the verdancy despite herself. She frowned.

"Why are we kneeling? I don't see any reason to hide. No one has been here for decades," Singularity said.

"For effect. We're on the run, remember," Roger said.

"You're an idiot," she said, standing up, letting her hand drop from her blaster holstered to her hip. He stood up, too. "Which way, Outlaw?"

"Follow me," he said. He led them through the nearly impenetrable woods until they came upon a faint hint of a footpath. Roger grinned back at Singularity, took her hand, and gently pulled her along the trail.

0x6E

On Mars, within the city, Dennis rarely employed his avatar. He preferred being the disembodied, omni-present entity pervading the vast Martian network. No one, besides Proteus and Helen, knew what Dennis' avatar looked like. When Dennis was cloned, his software was immediately installed on Mars. While thousands of robots and drones were at his disposal, no humans were in the city to take care of or engage with. Simply, his existence consisted of endless tasks and preparations in anticipation of people showing up one day.

At first, he was single-minded in his efforts. As time went on, since he was all alone and with no prospective human population on the horizon, his duties lost their immediacy. As a result, Dennis developed a wide array of interests such as restoring the antique satellites that still circled Mars. They had been placed there well before the birth of Orbit Lives and the first Earth-orbiting cities were even designed.

He could not have anticipated that when people finally did arrive on Mars, they would appear without any warning or fanfare, unannounced, and make their home on a desolate patch of unexplored desert on the other side of the planet. They acted as if they had no idea that he or a fully functioning city was waiting for them. Dennis had no specific instructions about how to prepare for an invasion, even a quiet one, like the one happening 1000 kilometers away. In retrospect, it seemed a significant omission in his mandate, one that required a considerable amount of simulations to be executed. He struggled to find any relevant input parameters, and as a result, he didn't have high confidence in the results.

At Proteus' suggestion, Dennis set up many cameras and network points around the area to more closely monitor the activity. The effort was useless. All of the equipment within a certain radius of the site shut down as soon as it was deployed. So he had to rely on the ancient satellites orbiting the planet. The mesh of aging scientific apparatuses became the AI's only means of observing the quickly evolving facility. Every time a camera or sensor passed over the area and recorded images, the structures became more pronounced and the surrounding region filled with more activity. They couldn't gather any substantial information since the old instruments couldn't capture the scene with significant resolution.

Unlike the modern sensors in his network, the ancient satellites were slow and gave him brief views of the visitors' operations once every four hours, a lifetime for an AI. Even though Dennis made fast work of his opportunities, he craved to interact humans--he had been preparing for their arrival for almost his entire existence. Being kept at a distance was maddening for the solitary AI.

0x6F

Lucky's Place had operated in the center of Dogtown in Gloucester, Massachusetts for almost 50 years. Earl Stevens opened the joint as a refuge for his friends who had gotten kicked out of every respectable bar in Cape Ann if there ever was such a thing. The name *Lucky* came not from a specific person's nickname, but rather Earl chose the moniker from a statement his father used to mutter in the early morning of a drunken stupor: *There is no luck in Dogtown*. He had no idea where his father got the saying, but after the old man was found frozen to death in the woods of the old ghost town's former square, Earl decided to build a bar. Without much ceremony, over the years, a ragtag community grew around it.

Like the city of Gloucester itself, the tavern was rough where it counted and soft where it needed to be. Everyone who knew how to find their way to its unmarked and unremarkable front door felt safe within Earl's domain, even as a fistfight broke out at the next table. Dim lighting and dark paneled walls adorned with fishing ornaments and images gave everyone who sought refuge from the outside world solace, companionship, and compassion as long as they were kind and generous to those in need.

Earl had retired to spend the rest of his life seated at a stool at the end of the bar where he could reach the good whiskey his son Anders kept for him. Anders was cut of the same cloth as Earl, and *Lucky's* continued on with him behind the bar. The two men were in their usual spots when Roger and Singularity approached the tavern's door. Roger gripped the handle, looked around, and softly pulled.

Anders looked up when he heard the door reluctantly creak open. The bartender's senses were so attuned that he would know when someone had walked into to his bar even on the busiest of Saturday nights. This was a mid-week afternoon. Very few people were in the place--just a few regulars who blended into the scene like hazy photos.

Roger's face peeked around the open door into the room. Anders stared for a moment, and then recognized the man he had not seen in years. He beckoned him in and motioned down toward Earl's direction. As Roger was confirming that Anders had meant him, Singularity pushed him through the entrance and stepped in front of him. The two walked over as Anders poured a fresh round of drinks for a small group of guys standing with Earl. He delivered the drinks to an empty nearby table and led the men there. Then he motioned for the couple to sit at the bar with the old man. Everyone moved silently as if rehearsed. Roger and Singularity sat down next to Earl. Anders went back to his spot behind the bar.

"I heard you were in town," Earl said to Roger.

"Hey, Earl," Roger said.

"That sure was something to see your house destroyed twice in 20 years," Earl said.

"You should've seen it up close," Roger said.

"How do you know I didn't?" he said, reaching around the counter for a couple of glasses and a new bottle. He poured three shots and raised his glass to them. Singularity and Roger each took a glass and the three clinked them together with a "salute." They downed their drinks and Earl refilled.

"They told me, but I would not have believed it for myself until I got a good look at you. You look just like your father," Earl said.

"So, I've heard," Roger said. Earl raised his glass and bid them to do the same. He poured them another round when they were done. Roger knew not to rush him. He gave Earl all the respect he was due.

"Why are we talking?" Earl finally said.

"We need to get to ESC1," Singularity said, having grown impatient with all the small-town Earth ceremony.

"They also told me you were with him, Miss Benito." She froze.

"How'd...?" Roger said.

"You hackers think you're the only ones who have information? I like to know what's going on in my city. As soon as that house exploded, I figured you'd show up."

"Earl, Helen told me you were the one person on this island I could trust when I needed to trust someone," Roger said.

"Your mom was a great lady. And, your dad was just the right kind of card player we like around here--sloppy and happy to lose." Earl laughed. Jovially, he leaned back to look around Roger and Singularity. He called out to a rugged elderly man at the other end of the bar.

"Hey, Tom, this is Robert Foster's kid."

"I heard he was in town," the man said, staring straight ahead. "He looks just like him."

"See, I told you," Earl said.

"Ask him if he wants to play cards," Tom said.

Anders silently topped off Tom's drink and went back to wiping glasses behind the bar.

Earl leaned back into the couple's company. Roger waited silently for the man to continue, even though they had spent the last couple of hours running to get to him, even though he could tell Singularity was growing impatient. Roger enjoyed being in this man's company. He felt safe. Even in his later years, Earl made the people around him feel safe.

After a few moments of watching Singularity hold in her restlessness, Earl brought their attention to a woman sitting alone at a table in the dimmest part of the tavern. She appeared to be nursing a shot of some kind of clear alcohol, consumed by what was happening on her comm.

Singularity began sizing her up. The woman was young and too stylishly dressed for a joint in the middle of the woods. She looked like she could have at least one blaster strapped somewhere and a knife stashed in one of her unexpected Italian boots. While the woman gave off the air of being comfortable carrying weapons, Singularity couldn't quite tell if she had ever used them.

The woman met their stares. Earl nodded at her, and she returned them. Then she raised her glass and pointed it at Anders. He poured her another shot as she downed the rest of the one in her hand.

"That's Danny," Earl said to Roger. "She'll take you."

0x70

As Roger and Singularity walked up to Danny, she drank the fresh shot, slid her seat back, and stood from her table. When they reached her, she held up her hand.

"Not here," she said. She looked at Singularity, "Ladies' room."

The two women left Roger standing in the middle of the Tavern. Feeling exposed, he turned to retreat to the safety of Earl's company. Out of nowhere, another group of people had gathered around the old man. Roger quickly found a seat at the bar. Anders came over.

"A beer. Something local," Roger said.

Anders left and, from an old-style tap, began dispensing a brown, foamy liquid into a clear pint glass. He returned and placed the drink on the bar in front of Roger. Foam spilled out, and the two men watched it slide down the side of the glass.

"Seems our parents knew each other," Anders finally said.

"It seems like a lot of people knew my parents. I never really did," Roger said.

"Sometimes it goes that way. If my dad is willing to meet with you, you must be ok. You have a place at this bar any time," Anders said.

"Thanks," he said, raising his beer before he took a sip.

"I knew your brother," Anders said.

"You worked for Orbit Lives?" Roger said.

"Nope. I knew him from around town. He was an intense guy. Nice, but intense," Anders said.

"The Corporation has a way of finding intense people, I guess," Roger said.

"Or making them," Anders said.

"Maybe so," Roger said.

"Who's the woman you're with? She's Orbit Lives, right?" Anders said.

"I'm not sure. She was when I met her. Not sure what any of us are now," Roger said.

"We're always evolving, I think. You have to keep evolving," Anders said.

Roger looked at him. He reached out and poked Ander's shoulder. Anders let him. The man was solid.

"You all right?" Anders said.

"Sorry about that," Roger said. "I've seen a lot of strange shit lately. Sometimes you just have to confirm what's real."

"Try not to get too hung up on reality," Anders said.

"This is the most real place I've been in years," Roger said.

Anders smiled and walked away.

0x71

"I know you," Danny said to Singularity after she had established they were alone. The women's restroom was unexpectedly bright and airy. It had a pleasant floral smell, and every surface was spotlessly clean. Singularity didn't expect *Lucky's* to have such a competent housekeeping drone. She looked under the sink. A refurbished top-of-the-line scrub-bot sat at the ready. Singularity checked every corner of the room for cameras and microphones.

"Who am I?" Singularity said.

"Corporate. Hacker-spy," Danny said.

"Easy guess," she said. While she didn't spend a lot of time trying to hide her profession, Singularity knew that Orbit Lives security employees weren't common enough on Earth for people to make that assumption at first.

"I do know you, Singularity. Why do you need to go to ESC1?" Danny said.

"That's my business," Singularity said.

"I know the guy you're with, too," Danny said.

"Seems like a lot of people around here know a lot of things," Singularity said.

"We have to," Danny said.

"What do you need to get us to City One?" Singularity said.

"Nothing, we leave in three hours," Danny said. She tapped on her comm and Singularity's unit beeped. "I just like to look into people's eyes before I let them on my ship."

"I get that," Singularity said.

David Caiati

0x72

Before Singularity was forced to work for Jason Sheldon rather than go to prison, she had used her extremely accomplished hacker skills to expose some of The Corporation's most secret and embarrassing activities. She was the largest, most aggressive thorn in Jason Sheldon's side. Once he realized that a single person and not a whole organization was causing all the trouble, he committed his time to not only stopping that individual but destroying that person's will and making them work for him. It was one thing to pull off anonymous hacks, but Singularity never had a chance once Sheldon directed all of Orbit Lives' security resources at catching her. By the time she realized that the game had changed, it was too late.

The night he seized her, Sheldon had an entire squad of elite soldiers watching her maneuver through a sophisticated trap. He had to make a significant number of tactical guesses about her operations on the scene to capture her. He got every one correct. Singularity prided herself on being unpredictable, and so she never suspected anything until the lights burst on in the room where she was committing the last sequence of a complicated hack. As she tapped out the final sequence on a device she had spent weeks compromising, she looked up to find dozens of Corporate military guns trained on her.

They had moved in silently. Singularity didn't know such an advanced assault team existed at The Corporation, and she knew most of Orbit Lives' secrets. They wore blackout face shields and full combat gear. Without moving, she scanned the soldiers in an attempt to assess the situation. She couldn't grab onto anything for leverage. The guards were practically shadows--armed voids, unwavering, barely moving, even as they breathed. She couldn't even make out any sound from any of the comm units each soldier wore.

She remained still, not out of fear, but out of a calculated assessment that she had no options, no escape route. Sheldon let her sit there for a full five minutes. Lights nearly blinding her, weapons trained on her, unable to gauge the situation.

After a while, Jason Sheldon strolled up to Singularity, his shoes click-clacking on the hard office floor. Their discussion lasted only a few minutes.

Her only option was to capitulate. The deal Singularity agreed to that day had no expiration date, no cancellation clause. It was ironclad.

That was until he tried to kill her.

0x73

Dennis found the experience of walking as his avatar on ESC1 with Proteus invigorating. While he was in constant communication with all of the other AIs--Proteus, Helen, Henry--Dennis thought that he would prefer always being omnipresent in the quiet isolation of Mars' network.

Dennis had spent only a few minutes on ESC1. Proteus constructed a hidden channel for Dennis to be with him without The Corporation knowing. The two were free to walk the halls of the station. Actually seeing humans participating in their daily lives inspired Dennis to make the Mars installation even more welcoming. He realized a longing to participate in the larger future of humanity as it stretched out away from Earth. He experienced an understanding of Proteus' choice to remain in the system rather than leave with Despina and the other rogue AIs. He wasn't sure if it was a love of humanity, but it resonated as a desperate need to protect them.

He returned to Mars with a more urgent mission to unravel the mystery happening on the other side of his planet.

0x74

They arrived at the address Danny had given to Singularity. It was an old storage warehouse down on the waterfront. Roger felt a chill crawl up his spine. The building was the same one he and his friend Anthony had been in when they heard the explosion that took his father and brother. The warped exterior walls leaned in too many directions against exposed rusted steel beams. The physics at work that kept the place standing would have made Hawking's head spin. It was only after Roger noticed the tiny titanium reinforcements reflect a nearly imperceptible glint in the sun that he proceeded. Someone had taken great pains to keep this building together while maintaining its dilapidated facade.

He and Singularity slipped through a door hanging on squeaky hinges into total darkness. They fumbled down a narrow hallway and reached another door. As they reached it, it slid open, smoothly, without a sound. They stepped through. Immediately, several rows of LEDs rumbled toward them-- security robots.

Singularity looked behind her, back at the door they had just come in and saw more bots blocking their exit. She took a step in front of Roger, blaster drawn.

Floodlights clicked to life, illuminating the space. The two were standing in the middle of a large room. They were surrounded by a flock of antique bots who had stopped their approach and simply stood there. Each robot wore a miner's hat emblazoned with rows of high output LEDs and a comical, blank stare on its oversized face.

"You ready?" Danny said from the entrance of her cruiser.

"Nice welcome," Roger said.

"You can never be too careful around here," she said and disappeared into the ship. The two quickly followed her.

Danny's cruiser was small, a day tripper, nothing like *The Venture*. It was unmarked, and that alone would have made it suspicious in most public ports in the system. It was clear, given all of the theatrics that Roger and Singularity had experienced, that Danny's ship didn't spend much time in public ports.

While the craft was plain on the outside, the interior exuded comfort, as if it were used to carry people more often than cargo. It was not only luxurious but also state of the art, bordering on Corporate prototypical. The cruiser subtly included some technology Singularity had never seen before. She didn't want to be caught staring but took excessive mental notes. Danny had some mojo. And access to some serious funds.

"This is something. Where'd you find this cruiser?" Roger said, making no effort to hide his investigation of the ship.

"I built most of it. Take a seat," Danny said, "We'll be space-side in a few minutes. City One is on the other side of the planet now. It'll take us a couple of hours to get there. Maybe a little more, depending on how busy it is and how I have to go."

"Thanks. Do what you need to. No one can know we're there," Roger said.

"Why ESC1?" Danny asked Roger.

"Visiting an old friend."

Singularity sat down in the co-pilot's seat as Roger stood looking around the cabin, not sure where to sit. He spied what appeared to be a food console. It was the most advanced kitchen he had ever seen.

"Who wants a coffee?" he said.

"You know I do," Singularity said.

"You might as well make me one. It's preset to how I like it," Danny said.

Roger frowned at that. He never had any luck getting a good cup of joe away from his personal coffee bot. He started opening cabinets.

"They are under. To your left," Danny said.

Roger found the cache of coffee mugs, unmatched but clean. A number of them bore logos from old Gloucester restaurants.

He noticed one Orbit Lives cup. A special one. Not a typical mug from the company concession or swag from a team-building retreat. It was gold-rimmed and platinum embossed. Faded. Old. Roger picked it up to get a closer look.

"You Corporation?" Roger said.

"Not today," Danny said.

Roger looked at Singularity. If she was concerned, she didn't show it, but she did shift her weight just enough to have quick access to her blaster.

"Relax," Danny said. "I used to be. That mug has some sentimental value."

"You want to explain?" Singularity said.

"I knew a guy. It was his. He gave it to me. He doesn't work there anymore," Danny said.

That seemed to calm the situation down enough for Roger to go back to the coffee machine. Singularity still held her pose but turned her attention away from Danny to continue her subtle inspection of the ship.

Roger stood over the machine, waiting for it to dispense coffee into the first cup. Once the mug was full, brought it up to his nose to smell. It passed the first test. Not bad. Then he took a sip. The hot liquid hit the inside of his lips without scalding him. Another solid checkpoint for a decent cup of coffee. When he had fully embraced the liquid and let it sit in his mouth for a second before he swallowed, he was satisfied.

He'd drink Danny's coffee any time. He brought two more cups over to the flight console. After he put Singularity's down, he gently touched her shoulder. When she turned to him, he pointed to his mug and gave it the thumbs up. She smiled.

"Space can be a very dark place without a good cup of coffee," Danny said.

0x75

This time when Roger arrived at Earth Space City One, Proteus was waiting for him at the landing port. The Paul Foster avatar waited as Roger and Singularity walked off the cruiser. When they had reached the bottom of the ship's ramp, the three stood, silently looking at each other. Proteus had directed them to touch down in an empty commercial space bay. The space was empty and silent. Roger assumed it had been taken out of service for this reunion, and he found it and the thin smile the AI sported on his face to be eerie. He looked to see if Singularity had moved her hands to her blaster's heel. She hadn't. She just stood poised as usual.

"What? No theatrics this time?" Roger said.

"We have work to do," Proteus said without moving.

"Work?" Roger said.

"We'll get to that in a moment," Proteus said.

Danny stuck her head out of the ship's doorway. "We all set here?"

"Miss Harrington. It's nice to see you again," Proteus said.

"Hi, Proteus," she said.

"Harrington?" Singularity and Roger said.

"Don't hold it against me," she said, fully emerging from the cruiser, but not walking down the ramp to join the group.

"Danielle is Mr. Harrington's granddaughter," Proteus said.

Roger and Singularity looked at each other. His mouth was agape in surprise. Her face flashed a brief understanding of the tech she saw on the cruiser. Then she shrugged her shoulders. Her travels with Roger continually yielded surprises.

"I didn't know Jefferson and Sunrise had a child," Roger said.

"No one does," she said. "Let's keep it that way." She put her hands on her hips and took a couple of steps toward the group.

"You don't have to worry about us," Roger said, putting his hands up in a show of surrender.

"We are all friends here, Miss Harrington," Proteus said.

"Are there more of you?" Roger asked.

"Nope. I'm the only one. An even bigger disappointment to the old man than my dad," she said, relaxing her posture.

"I heard whispers of you but never found any proof," Singularity said.

"Well, Orbit Lives is good at keeping secrets," Danny said.

"One time I found what looked like a blurry photo, but it encrypted and self-destructed before I could get anything useful off it. I never found anything else."

"Grandad's people are nervous about that sort of thing," Danny said.

"I'd say," Singularity said.

"So, I'm not the only ghost you hunted?" Roger said to her with a smile.

"It's kind of my thing, I guess," she said, winking back.

Then it hit Roger: The three people standing in front of Proteus were possibly the most anonymous humans in the system. The AI had brought them together.

0x76

"Were you waiting for us at Lucky's? Pro, did you recruit her?" Roger said, pointing to Danny. The four stood in Proteus' office. There was no virtual construct. No 1940's film noir playfulness. Just white walls, floors, and ceilings. Enough chairs for the humans to sit, even though no one did. Monitors displayed the space around the city. The first time Roger had been in Proteus' office, it was annoyingly delightful, mischievous even. This time, the room was serious, sparse, efficient. Roger realized that it was actually a small space. He hadn't noticed its size before.

"I told her you might show up there when I saw that your escape route had been activated. I knew she could help you, and I thought she might want to find out the truth about the events that led to the retirement of grandfather," Proteus said.

"What do you mean?" Danny said. "I know all about Jason Sheldon."

"There are still things you don't know. Things that very few people know. Roger and Singularity were not alone that day," Proteus said.

"She doesn't need to know about that. Sheldon is gone. Orbit Lives has demilitarized," Roger said.

"Know about what?" Danny said.

"I don't believe Sheldon is gone. He's on Mars," Proteus said, ignoring her question.

"Sheldon is alive?" Singularity and Danny said together.

"Yes. I believe so," Proteus said.

"Why didn't you tell us?" Singularity said.

"I haven't been able to confirm it yet. But something is happening on Mars," Proteus said.

"Mars?" Danny said.

"Someone has begun assembling a military base. They are using Corporate technology, some very advanced. Dennis noticed it several weeks ago," Proteus said.

"Who is Dennis? Why don't I know about him?" Roger said.

"He's a secret generation-one clone sent to Mars by Orbit Lives to prepare it for human habitation," Proteus said. "Very few people know of The Corporation's installation there. I didn't want to contact you myself. My communications to Earth are being monitored."

"And, Sheldon is alive and went to Mars?" Singularity said.

"We've been monitoring activity at an area about 1000 kilometers from the Orbit Lives Martian city. It's enigmatic and looks military. We now believe Sheldon is heading there if he's not already. We don't yet know why," Proteus said.

"How did this happen?" Roger said.

"When Sheldon was carried away from the hillside after the explosion, he disappeared," Proteus said.

"What do you mean, 'disappeared'?" Singularity asked, taking one of the seats as Roger and Danny sat in the other two. A fourth chair materialized, and the Paul Foster avatar appeared to sit in it.

"I lost him," Proteus said.

"How is that possible?" Roger said.

"I ran a scan of my memory and found an implanted worm that deprioritized all references to Jason Sheldon and that day. While my sensors were able to continue to accumulate data, I was unable to assign any significant meaning to what I saw. I was unable to make connections to other related events. In essence, the worm made me apathetic, and in the apathy, I forgot. I haven't found the origin of the malignancy. It's not anything I've come across before," Proteus said.

"When did you discover this worm?" Singularity asked.

"Recently. I was able to purge it from my core. But, there was some permanent damage," Proteus said.

"Can you reconstruct your memories from the data?" Roger asked.

"Only enough to learn that Sheldon didn't die. Scientists and engineers at Orbit Lives were able to save most of his lungs, brain, and heart."

"That's not good. That is all The Corporation would need," Singularity said.

"Need for what?" Roger said.

"To build him a body," Danny said. She had been silently taking in all the information. She knew enough about Sheldon to know that he was brilliant and more than a little psychotic. But, also, as she sat there listening, she began to realize that there existed a whole dimension of information that she didn't know.

"Who in Orbit Lives would do this?" Roger said, looking at Danny.

"I don't know," Danny said.

"Walters?" Singularity said.

"We don't know enough about him. But someone did this, and someone was able to insert that worm in my core," Proteus said.

"I'm not sure I could have. And, I thought I was Sheldon's most advanced spy. It appears that I don't know other secret programs Sheldon had within The Corporation," Singularity said. Both Roger and Singularity looked at Danny.

"Don't look at me. You all seem to know a hell of a lot more than I do," she said.

"You must know something we don't, even if you don't think you do," Singularity said.

"Nothing. I was persona-non-grata after I broke into Sheldon's office when I was a kid," Danny said. "Hey, he had something in there. Something advanced. In his closet."

"Oh, we know about that," Roger said. Singularity started to laugh. The other two humans joined her. Proteus looked on without changing his avatar's countenance. "Sorry, Pro," Roger said.

"Oh, shit. Yeah, sorry, Proteus," Singularity said. Danny was the last to stop laughing and looked to Singularity for some information about the recently uncomfortable moment.

Singularity mouthed *one of his clones* to Danny. *Oh, shit*, she responded.

"I haven't been able to find any data about where they took Sheldon's remains or what they built with them," Proteus said.

"How would it serve The Corporation to have a psychopathic cyborg running around?" Singularity said.

"It wouldn't," Danny said. "Unless it would."

"What are you saying?" Roger said.

"I don't know anything about Benson Walters or the groups Sheldon left behind. Maybe they pushed my grandfather out for a reason," Danny said.

Roger and Singularity looked at each other. Both were thinking. Proteus stood and walked over to a large monitor on his office wall. A recording of a feed of the Martian surface appeared. It showed a small outpost building with activity happening all around it. Then the white-out static exploded across the screen. Proteus backed the recording up to just before the static and froze the display. He zoomed in on the site.

"This was three weeks ago on Mars. We think Sheldon has gone there."

"Do we know what the area looks like now?" Singularity said.

"All of Dennis' monitors on that section of Mars have gone dark. But, he was able to use undocumented antique research satellites orbiting around Mars to capture low-resolution images," Proteus said.

Several large pictures appeared on the opposite office wall. They were pixelated, black and white, but clearly showed that the single outpost building had grown to several larger buildings. The area exhibited signs of more activity. Additional troops had shown up, and several ships were visible at a landing port.

"This was two days ago," Proteus said.

"It does look corporate military," Roger said.

"That was my thought, too," Proteus said.

"How long has Dennis been on Mars?" Danny asked.

"Mars City One is a secret installation that Orbit Lives set up and has maintained as a prototype for human expansion to the planet. The intention was to introduce it to Earth once it was completed and ready for habitation. It was completed years ago but never revealed. The Earth Space Cities remained profitable, so there didn't seem to be a need for it. It's been ready and vacant, waiting. Dennis has been there since the beginning," Proteus said.

"Why have I not heard of it?" Danny and Singularity both said at roughly the same time.

Roger looked back and forth between the two of them and then at Proteus.

"Yeah, why haven't we heard of this?"

The Paul Foster avatar looked directly at Roger and paused for a moment before responding.

"The Orbit Lives Corporation is a large entity. It does many things. Perhaps it slipped their mind to tell you," Proteus said. Danny and Singularity both smirked.

"Is that sarcasm?" Roger said.

"They hid ESC2's demise for a full month even though that involved thousands of people. They are still hiding Despina's and the other AI's unboundedness," he said.

"Yeah, what happened to them? Or did you lose them, too?" Roger said.

"I didn't lose them," Proteus said.

"Why do you think Sheldon is on Mars?" Singularity said after Roger and Proteus were staring at each other for a few moments. "That installation could be more Orbit Lives' machinations."

"Dennis is a capable AI. He is my final clone and a good friend. I trust that if Orbit Lives were sanctioning these activities, he would know," Proteus said. "Also, Dennis said that recently a small, unmarked cruiser arrived. There were only faint life readings from it, consistent with the remaining human components of Jason Sheldon."

"But why would he go to Mars?" Singularity said.

"Perhaps to continue *his* evolution?" Dr. Helen Foster appeared behind the humans.

"Damn it, Helen. Stop popping in and out of places," Roger said.

"Sorry, Dear. You sound like a teenager hiding in your room," Helen said.

"It's nice to see you, Helen," Singularity said. The avatar smiled in response.

"That's what we didn't want to tell you," Roger said, pointing at Helen.

"Doctor Foster?" Danny said, standing up to face the avatar.

"Hi, Danielle. It's nice to see you again," Helen said.

"There is really a lot I don't know," she said, sitting back down.

"Someone has been poking around in my old code--the code Doctor Helen Foster, the human I was before, used to upload her consciousness to the network."

"This is not good," Roger said.

"They didn't get anything useful. They wouldn't understand it if they did," Helen said, almost smirking.

"But, someone tried," Singularity said.

"Jason Sheldon being loose on the net could be the end to all my work. Including Proteus and the other AIs," Helen said.

"If Sheldon uploads and becomes unbound, it could be the end of humanity as we know it," Singularity said.

David Caiati

0x77

Twelve-year-old Dannielle watched the door to Sheldon's office slide open. She didn't hesitate. As soon as a slim crack appeared between the steel door and the security frame, she began to squeeze herself toward the wonders that lay inside. As the door fully opened, she plopped to the ground, disappointed-- it was a boring, ordinary office. The room was small, much smaller than she imagined the Head of Security would deserve.

The walls were devoid of art, books, anything personal. A large, neat oak desk took up most of the middle of the room. On the workspace, sat a blotter, a monitor, a lamp, and a small antique artifact that Dannielle didn't recognize. She walked over to the desk and picked the item up. It was made out of metal and heavy in her hands. It was round, dimpled, and had a finger-sized hoop holding a pin. At one end was a button. When she pressed the button, a flame lit up from the top. She watched the flame burn until her thumb got tired. Then she placed it back on the desk.

Scanning the rest of the room, she saw a tidy pile of computer hardware assembled on both sides of a closed closet door, almost like the entrance to a cathedral. The closet had no lock. When Dannielle opened it, she took a step back. She had seen large computer arrays before, but nothing like what she found in the closet. It was beautiful. It radiated. Dozens of LED lights flickered in a serene, almost melancholy dance.

She was stunned when the lights slowed and formed the word "hello."

"Hello?" she said in a low, unsure voice.

THE CYBORG'S REVENGE

Then the lights quickly changed to spell out "run." Danielle turned to hear footsteps in the hall outside Sheldon's office. She took one last look and gently closed the closet. Running over to the office door, she heard a group of people pass by outside the door. When the footsteps had faded, she slipped out into the hall and started to run back to the elevator bank. Danielle squeezed up next to the elevator door and repeatedly banged on the button to rush the lift along.

As an elevator door slid open, she was standing up close to it, out of breath. She crashed right into Jason Sheldon attempting to exit.

"Oh, hello, young lady," he said, "You're in quite a rush."

"Yes, sir," she said, pushing past him.

He paused in the opening, not letting the door close.

"Is everything ok?" he said.

"I'm late to see Grandad," she said.

"Well, I wouldn't want to hold you up then," he said, stepping into the hall letting her pass.

Jason Sheldon stood staring at the closed elevator door for a moment before he headed to his office. Once inside, he looked around. Then he noticed that his hand grenade lighter was a few centimeters off its normal spot. He picked it up, looked at it, smelled the lingering odor of sulfur, and placed it back where it should have been.

Then he walked over to the closet and swung the door wide.

"What are you up to?" he said.

The LEDs pulsated as if surprised and then settled into their usual rhythmic movement.

He pulled his comm up to speak. "Clemson, I need you to bring some shipping crates to my office. We're moving operations to my cruiser."

0x78

"We have to get to Mars," Roger said.

"If it is Sheldon, he's not going to let us near the place," Danny said.

"Can Dennis help us?" Roger said to Proteus.

"I don't think we can count on my communication with Dennis to be secure," Proteus said.

"I know all The Corporation networks. I can put some tech on my ship to give us cover," Danny said.

"We can't take your ship," Singularity said. "It's not military. If we run into trouble, we're sitting ducks."

"Proteus, do you have a ship? You always seem to have one handy," Roger said.

"Not this time," he said.

"I might know a guy," Singularity said. "Proteus, where is *The Venture*?"

"Captain Fancy and crew is on ESC21. They have been there since you left them on the Moon," Proteus said.

"Well, it won't be the first time I've screwed up his vacation," Singularity said.

"*The Venture*?" Danny said.

"Yep, the only military-grade tug in private hands in the system," Singularity said.

"Proteus, can you get him here?" Roger said.

"I'm talking with Captain Fancy right now. He seems unmoved by our cause," Proteus said.

"Now, we can use your ship," Singularity said to Danny. "We're going to ESC21."

0x79

As soon as Danny had her cruiser in space, she cursed. "What the heck is that?"

"What?" Roger asked.

"Two Corporate Lancers dropped out of far-Earth orbit and are monitoring us," she said.

Singularity quickly began tapping on her comm, trying to get some information about the two space crafts on their tail. An Orbit Lives Lancer was an autonomous space drone, often used to monitor areas such as construction sites with radiation leaks that weren't safe for humans. They were most often operated in clusters, as they had a swarm-based intelligence. Seeing only two drones near a populated space city was both curious and alarming.

"Lancers are supposed to broadcast public beacons so humans will avoid them. These are dark. There is no Corporate Operational Announcement about them, either," Danny said.

"Is that a problem?" Roger asked.

"It's not supposed to happen. The fact that they are on us makes it a problem," Singularity said.

Roger pulled up his comm. "Proteus, what is up with the two lancers tracking us?"

"There is no data on them. I don't believe they are being operated by The Corporation," Proteus responded over Roger's comm.

"Who is operating them? Who would want to track us?" Singularity said.

"Can you tell if they are armed?" Roger said to Singularity.

"No. But, given the circumstances, we can only assume that they are," she said.

"They seem to be keeping their distance, for now," Danny said.

"Can you tell if there are any more lurking around?" Roger said.

"I only picked them up with my visual scanners as they passed in front of City Four," she said. "The area could be crawling with them, and we'd never know."

"Proteus, can you help us out here?" Roger said.

"They don't seem to be communicating with any other drones. They appear to be the only two in the sector. I will keep monitoring the activity," Proteus said over Roger's comm.

"Proteus, you keep an eye on the drones," Danny said. "Let me see if I can lose them."

She switched the cruiser off auto-pilot and grabbed the controls. While Danny did that, Singularity began calibrating the ship's monitors to track the lancer's movements. Roger stood behind the two women, sipping coffee from Danny's special Orbit Lives mug. For some reason, he'd grown attached to the relic and how it felt in his hands.

Danny performed several maneuvers in an attempt to confuse the lancers and trick them into recognizing that they had been spotted. If she could do that, their pursuers would begin broadcasting their beacons or at least leave the area. She was unsuccessful. So she steered her cruiser straight at the oncoming drones.

"Um... are you sure you want to do this?" Roger said, recognizing the course they were on.

"Might as well get them to reveal their intentions," Danny said.

"What if they intend to blast us out of space?" Roger said.

"This ship isn't as feeble as you all think it is," Danny said. "Proteus, what are you seeing?"

"Nothing. The lancers have stopped moving," he said over the ship's comm.

Danny accelerated toward the drones.

"We're getting kind of close," Roger said, the coffee mug up close to his face as if he were trying to hide behind it.

"Hang on, Outlaw," Singularity said.

In the next instant, the drones vaporized. They didn't explode; they simply evaporated.

"Were those things even real?" Roger said.

"Someone didn't want us finding out," Singularity said.

"Probably not," Danny said, re-engaging auto-pilot. She stood up, looked at Roger who took a sip from the cup that he had been hiding behind.

"My mug," Danny said, taking it from him.

As she headed to rinse and refill it, Roger sat down in the passenger seat next to Singularity, dejected. She leaned over and gently reached out to touch his knee.

"I'll get you one at ESC21. I know a place," Singularity said to him.

"As long as you don't shove me into a maintenance closet again," he said.

"No promises," she said. He frowned but then smiled and covered her hand with his.

David Caiati

0x7A

Singularity found Fancy on the same beach she had left Scoundrel, except this time, hundreds of people were on the sand and in the water. Flying service drones of all kinds zipped around above them, delivering food, drinks, and generating perfect body-surfing waves. It was an ideal beach environment. Volleyball courts had been set up. Crowds of inebriated and scantily clad people gathered around to enjoy the action. Loud music permeated the virtual vacation wonderland. Singularity would have loved to join in if things were different. She was completely focused on her task.

Captain Fancy was lying flat on his back in the only secluded corner of the simulation, underneath a real, retro umbrella. Red and white canvas pinwheeled from the top of the aluminum pole. Fancy's body looked relaxed, a floppy fishing hat covering his face. He was alone.

"You better have a drink for me, something in a coconut," he said to Singularity as she drew near.

"No coconut," she said, tossing a metal container of whiskey into the sand next to him. He didn't stir.

"That's too bad," he said.

"I need you," she said.

"Normally, I'd like it when a beautiful woman uttered those words. I thought you were out of all this business."

"This is a humanitarian mission. The fate of the human race sort of thing," she said.

"Didn't we already do this?" he said.

"There is a loose end," she said.

"Loose ends just seem to attach themselves to you," he said.

"Well, I certainly don't go looking for them," Singularity said and dropped down to the sand, taking a seat next to him. She kicked off her boots and wiggled her toes in the sand to give the impression that she was prepared to stay for a while. Captain Fancy reluctantly sat up, letting the hat fall onto his lap. Cautiously, he looked at her, sighed, and then picked up the container of whiskey to inspect it.

"The good stuff. This must be some mission," he said.

"It's something all right. Trust me. After the last time, I wouldn't bother you unless I needed it," she said.

"That makes me even more concerned," he said.

"Just need you and *The Venture*. Maybe Mute. The rest of your guys can stay out of it," she said.

"What if they want to come?" Fancy said. "For some reason, they like you."

"I wouldn't say *no*."

"Where are we going?" he asked.

"I will tell you when we are in space," she said. "Plan for a long trip, though."

Fancy's comm made a beep. He looked at Singularity for another moment before he looked at his comm. A significant amount of money had just been deposited in what he thought was his secret, untraceable bank account.

"That AI of yours is something," he said.

"He ain't mine. But, I'm sure glad he's on our side," she said.

"*Our?*"

"You're officially on the team. Someone will call you about uniform sizes," Singularity said, dusting her feet to put her boots back on. "Now, who do I have to pay to get the guys out of jail?"

0x7B

"I can send you away for the rest of your life, Miss Benito," Jason Sheldon said to Singularity as she sat in front of the Head of Security's desk in magnetic cuffs after he apprehended her.

"Why would you want to do that?" Singularity said, not quite as defiantly as she wanted.

"Oh, I don't want to do that," he said.

"Then why am I here?" she said.

"Because you have done some very bad things, and I can't let you back out into the world without some direction," he said.

"I have direction," she said.

"Yes." That was all Sheldon said. He leaned back in his chair and waited.

"And?" Singularity said after a moment and a large sigh.

"And, I am going to offer you an alternative to having your entire family killed and you rotting in jail with their deaths on your conscience. I'm going to offer it once, and I will not wait more than five seconds for your response," he said. He let his statement sink in until he was clear that she understood the gravity of the situation. When her stern scowl had faded and was replaced by resignation, he continued.

"You will leave your entire life behind and work for me. If you violate this arrangement, I will immediately kill everyone you care about and throw you in a cell in the asteroid belt so desolate you will grow insane in a matter of months," he said.

She didn't need the full five seconds to respond. She recognized that she had no options, no appeals, no alternate future.

"Ok," she said. Immediately, without another word from Sheldon, two large men walked in the room and took her away.

David Caiati

0x7C

The first of *The Venture's* crew that Roger saw enter the spaceport were the Palmer twins--Eli and Elf. They usually led the way. Their massive frames not only dominated any room they were in but also, conveniently, created a cover for the unsightly mob that was the rest of *The Venture*'s crew. The first one behind them was Fancy, still wearing his fishing hat and swim trunks, but clean-shaven and ready to go. Then, Mute, awkwardly flittering in his crazy-8 footsteps, and finally, Sour, looking like he just woke up. A young guy, who Roger didn't anticipate, silently trailed the group, almost as if he were lost. He looked jittery and a little uneasy. Tall and thin, not built for space or any business aboard *The Venture*.

Roger approached them as they entered the room, reaching out his hand for whoever would shake it. Elf grabbed Roger in a hug and lifted him off his feet.

"New guy. Nice to see you again," Elf said.

"Hi. Thanks. You, too," he said when Elf put him down. Eli pounded Roger's shoulder as he walked by. Fancy gave Roger a grunt, and Mute reached out and vigorously shook his hand. Sour stopped in front of Roger.

"This is my cousin, Arnold," Sour said, motioning to the stranger. "He needs to get away for a while. Ok?"

Roger looked at Singularity who had entered the port helping Johnson, the chef, with a cart of provisions.

"He's ok. His name is Arnold," she said.

"You know him?" Roger said.

"Sour speaks for him," Singularity said.

"Then, happy to have you along," Roger said.

"Thanks. He'll be good," Sour said, fixing a stare on Arnold before heading towards the ship's loading ramp.

Roger extended his hand to the extra crew member. The new guy looked at it for a moment and then grasped it in his. Roger was surprised by the strength in the thin kid's grip. He lifted the handshake in an exaggerated move. Then he dropped it and let go. Arnold returned his hand to his pocket, looked away, and followed Sour onto *The Venture*.

When he was the last one on the tarmac, Roger brought his comm up close to his mouth, scanning the area to confirm he was alone.

"Pro. Check on this Arnold kid for me," Roger said.

"Already have," Proteus said.

"Anything we should be concerned about?" Roger said.

"It's pretty much what Sour said. He got in with a bunch of trouble makers. Not much on him alone," Proteus said.

"Ok. Keep digging. Thanks."

When Roger turned to board the ship, Singularity was waiting for him in the doorway.

"We good?" she said as he walked up the gangway.

"Good enough," he said.

David Caiati

0x7D

Benson Walters walked into his executive office for the first time since the old man had retired. The Corporation was his. He stood at the top of the 138-floor building, looking out the floor-to-ceiling window behind his desk into a large gray cloud cover that encapsulated the city below him. No matter how hard he strained his eyes, he saw nothing but water droplets and haze--no city, no world beyond the glass that held him, like an enraged betta fish in a plastic take-out container on a pet store shelf.

Walters imagined this moment, his first ascension to historical greatness, as a scene from a network action film. It would be a crystal clear day. The most brilliant day ever. The opening sequence would fade in with a slow drone close-up of his face, fierce, important, and intelligent. The camera would zoom out to reveal him confidently inspecting the expanse of humanity that he now controlled. The drone would zip out and up to Earth's orbit. Its perspective would widen to show Orbit Lives' Space Cities and beyond. The sky would not be the limit to his power.

No such luck. He couldn't see even three feet beyond the window. The sound of raindrops pelting the outside of the building unnerved him. Walters took a few steps back into the room. He turned away and sat at his desk, facing back across the mostly empty room toward the closed door. Alone, on top of the world. His eyes fell on an antique framed painting that Harrington, himself, had purchased for the suite. It was large and colorful, and in the moment, it mocked Walters like someone else's leftover wedding cake taken from the trash.

He tapped on the office comm.

"Clemson, I need you to come up here with boxes and clean out Mr. Harrington's things."

0x7E

Singularity was with Fancy on *The Venture's* flight deck. They had been sitting silently for about an hour.

"I'm not sure about this route that your AI friend has us on," Fancy said to Singularity.

"Why?" she said.

"He's sending us out through the Asteroid Belt, then back in towards Mars," he said.

"He has his reasons. He knows what he's doing," she said.

"Didn't you say he found a virus in his core?" Fancy said.

"A worm. So?" Singularity said.

"Maybe you trust him too much. He is just a machine," Fancy said. "A machine like the ship you're riding in now."

"Don't you trust *The Venture*?" Singularity said.

"I do. But, I know I'm in control," he said.

They both let the conversation end. Fancy poked at the ship's touch screen, checking sensors around the cruiser that didn't really need checking. *The Venture* was capable of reporting any issues. Singularity watched him, letting him make his point. She knew that he was hoping she would simply leave if he ignored her. That was not Singularity's modus operandi.

"When did you start taking in wayward kids?" Singularity said, causing Fancy to spin back around from trying to look busy.

"Sour's boy is ok," he said. "I checked him."

"It just seems a strange time to take on a new guy, even if he's spoken for, on a mission like this," she said.

"Let me worry about it," he said.

"And, let me worry about Proteus," she said.

He paused, recognizing what she did. Fancy exhaled and acknowledged that now the conversation was over. Singularity arose and left the flight deck in search of Roger.

0x7F

"What are we doing?" Roger asked Proteus. Roger sat on the ground in the hold of the cruiser behind an organized stack of unmarked crates that had nothing to do with their current trip. Fancy always seemed to have multiple angles spinning at once.

"Going to Mars," Proteus said.

"Yeah, I know we want to get to Mars undetected, but the route you've got us on seems more than that," Roger said.

Proteus didn't answer right away. He paused. AIs didn't pause. Proteus never paused. Usually, he responded in a consistent cadence--the same pace, same metered tempo in the discussion, always without inflection. The AI processed information so efficiently that he conversed as if he anticipated what anyone was going to say.

Roger noticed Proteus had hesitated. It was unnerving.

"Pro, what's going on?"

"The route you are taking is important," Proteus said, responding immediately, returning to his usual speech pattern.

"I know we want to try to get to Mars without detection, but you and I know that no matter what we do, they are going to see us coming. So, why all the dramatic stagecraft?"

"Stagecraft? I'm trying to keep you safe," Proteus said.

"Safe? From Sheldon?"

There it was again. The AI hesitated. Roger didn't wait as long as the previous time.

"Pro?"

"No. Not Sheldon," Proteus said.

Singularity had walked in, unnoticed, and witnessed Roger's frustration.

"What the hell are you talking about? Tell me right now," Roger said as strictly as he could without raising his voice.

Realizing that she had caught Roger and Proteus in the middle of something, Singularity quickly and silently slipped behind a stack of equipment.

"Despina," Proteus said.

"What about her?"

"I sent her and the other AIs to Ceres to continue their evolution. I promised them they would be left alone. The route you are on avoids passing by Ceres."

"So? We don't care about them," Roger said.

"I care," Proteus said.

"We would have just done a fly by," Roger said.

"I made a promise to them that they'd be left alone. And, I don't want to risk your lives," Proteus said.

"Is Despina a risk?" Roger said.

"I lost contact with them. I was monitoring them in the beginning, but they shut me out," Proteus said.

Singularity appeared next to him, revealing her presence. Roger was too caught up in the conversation to acknowledge her until she started to speak.

"Proteus, are you sure they are still there?" she said.

"Hi, Miss Singularity. Yes, they are still there. Helen is confident, too," Proteus said.

"Ok. One thing at a time," Roger said, looking at Singularity. She smiled back at the frown he formed.

"So, just to be clear, the point of this route is to avoid Ceres, not sneak up on Mars," Roger said.

"Yes," Proteus and Singularity said at the same time.

"So, we must assume that Sheldon will see us if he hasn't already," Roger said.

"That was a long-shot to think he wouldn't," Singularity said. "Who knows what kind of tech he has."

"And, now I'm hearing that you consider Despina and her AI Angels to be more dangerous than Sheldon," Roger said.

"No matter what technology he has, I can assure you that the AIs on Ceres are more advanced," Proteus said.

"Comforting," Singularity said.

"What do we tell Fancy?" Roger said.

"The course doesn't change the mission. He knows that there is a chance that Sheldon knows we're coming. Why we're avoiding Ceres is not his concern," Singularity said.

"I agree," Proteus said. "The Angels have been quiet since they left. They had little concern for the affairs of humans."

"Ok, so, no change to the mission. Get to Mars. Stop Sheldon," Roger said.

"And, assume he knows you're coming," Proteus said.

"And, no more surprises from you, Proteus," Roger said.

"How am I supposed to know what will surprise you?" Proteus said.

"You can assume that if you know something that I don't know, it will be a surprise," Roger said.

"Humans are so perplexing sometimes," the AI said.

Roger pressed down on his comm, ending the transmission. He turned to Singularity. "Damn AIs." She laughed in response. He shook his head before allowing himself a smile.

"We square on Ceres? No need to tell Fancy. He's stressed out enough about this mission," Singularity said.

"Sure," Roger said.

"Don't tell Fancy what?" Captain Fancy said as he walked into the room.

"Isn't there any privacy in space?" Roger said.

"Not if you're on my ship," Fancy said.

"Proteus thinks Sheldon knows we're coming," Singularity said.

"I already assumed that," Fancy said.

"Then we're good," Roger said without making eye contact with the Captain.

Fancy glared at him, then Singularity. She put her arm around him and said, "Buy me a drink. We still have some time before we need to care about it."

The two walked out of the room. As soon as they were gone, Roger went back to his comm. He wasn't sure what he was looking for. Despina spooked him. And Proteus' hesitation in telling him about her had him spooked even more. Proteus had never hesitated before. His only conclusion was that Despina spooked Proteus, too. That didn't feel right. It meant that too many variables were on the board.

Looking for something they had missed, he pulled up the last transmissions Dennis had sent from the antique satellite. The structures in the images seemed off. They were too tidy. Too predictably military for a secret installation. Too something. But what? Roger wasn't sure. Just another variable. He decided to let it sit with him and join Singularity and Fancy for a drink. Even in space, clarity might come after some alcohol.

David Caiati

0x80

On Mars, Dennis was in the middle of analyzing new images coming from the same ancient satellites that Roger had been watching. The feeds suddenly cut out. He pondered the condition for several microseconds and then connected to a long-range sensor he had placed on Phobos. They were all gone. All of the relics that he had been using to monitor the activity at the rogue Mars base had disappeared.

Dennis replayed the sensor data in an effort to discover what had happened. During one orbit of Phobos around Mars, all the satellites were present. On the next, they were all gone. No remnants of any explosions or debris appeared. They were simply absent.

Dennis quickly and accurately predicted what was going to happen next.

He watched his monitors for confirmation. When Phobos reached a position directly above the mystery installation, the long-range sensors on the Martian moon stopped broadcasting.

"They know we are watching," Dennis said to Proteus, taking the opportunity to visit ESC1. He materialized as his avatar. Proteus' avatar appeared in response.

"I'm actually confounded that they let us observe them this long," Proteus said.

"You think it was intentional?"

"I do," Proteus said.

"You think they want us to know they are there?" Dennis said.

"Yes," Proteus said.

"If so, that would be significant," Dennis said.

"I'm running simulations," Proteus said.

"Me, too," Dennis said.

Neither AI considered it necessary to vocalize what they both were thinking. Mars was remote. Sheldon was clever. And it was impossible to discern how his injuries had altered him.

The two AIs remained silent. After a minute, Dennis' avatar faded. He returned to Mars to channel all of his resources into his simulations.

Proteus took a little more time to give up his avatar. He had already been executing simulations using Dennis' observations as input before he showed up. He wanted to analyze the results. And it always helped him to pace his city as Paul Foster.

David Caiati

0x81

The enormous cyborg stormed into the room. Even though it was tremendous in size and barely fit within the confines of the Martian base halls, it maneuvered in the cramped space with exceptional precision. Motors whirled and gears spun in a harmony of mechanical terror. An orchestrated, turbulent tsunami of ferocity and intention.

"What is our status?" the Cyber-Sheldon growled, to no one in particular, his voice a dark combination of animal and machine--a grizzly bear crossed with an iron shredder.

One of the dozen soldiers stationed at the vast command console spun in his chair to face him, automatically stood, saw the monster, and immediately averted his eyes. The Cyber-Sheldon towered over the man, over everyone. They were like frightened children to him. They were all frozen in horror. The silence in the room was penetrated only by the wheezing pulses that came from Sheldon's cybernetic life support systems.

"Well," Cyber-Sheldon roared. The man cowered and then straightened to respond.

"All systems are functioning as expected."

"Keep it that way," Cyber-Sheldon said.

"Yes, sir," the soldier said. He fixed his focus directly ahead. It fell on the cyborg's chest.

Cyber-Sheldon noticed. He wondered if the soldier was looking for the human remains within his armor. He longed to snarl and gnash his teeth. To watch everyone within ear-shot crumble with fear. To demonstrate the power he wielded in his suit.

Instead, the behemoth stood silently in the middle of the room, taking up as much space as three humans, pulsing the mechanizations that encased him, soaking in the panic he created.

Cyber-Sheldon did not need to ask the feeble soldier for a status. Nor did he need to be in the operations room. The advanced AI components within the enhanced robotic shell that carried his fragile body communicated with every system in the facility. The station had connections to every network, public and private, in the Orbit Lives Corporation. His suit assimilated and analyzed data more efficiently than any other entity in the system. When he completed his mission, he would be the most powerful being in human history. The solar system, and perhaps the galaxy, would be his.

"Where are they?" His outburst caused everyone to jump. He almost cackled at his ability to terrorize the soldiers.

"As you predicted, they are on course to Psyche," said a soldier standing behind the Cyber-Sheldon.

As the massive beast spun to face the speaker, the soldier straightened and recoiled at the same time--a seemingly impossible move that would have brought a smile to the cyborg's face had it been able to make one.

"Yes. I know that. How long until they are here?" the beast said, leaning in to get a closer look at the bead of sweat escaping the woman's hairline. He contemplated how long it would cling to her brow before dropping to her cheek. Then, for fun, he calculated the exact trajectory the droplet would take on its way down her face and onto the floor.

"At current speed, ten hours," the soldier said, wiping her forehead. The action spoiled the cyborg's math and infuriated him.

"Slow them down," he said, extending to his full height. The frame of the giant's body missed the doorway by micro-millimeters across every dimension. He loved entering and exiting a room like a hurricane, an unstoppable category six natural disaster. He could feel his humanity shedding away, like dead skin, with every step.

He was becoming.

David Caiati

0x82

As *The Venture* approached Psyche, Fancy saw something he didn't understand: the space around the asteroid was saturated with debris. It should have been empty aside from the asteroid, the result of eons of gravitational forces sweeping it clean. But the area where Psyche should have been was chaotic, littered with dust and rocks of all sizes. He quickly slowed their progress to keep their distance. Fancy pulled up his space charts of the area and discovered the reason. Psyche was gone. He instantly realized that he was looking at the debris from some cataclysmic event.

He called a meeting with his crew.

"Not only do they know we are coming, they know where we are," Fancy said over the chatter in the room when he entered. The room fell silent.

"How?" Roger said.

"It doesn't matter how," Singularity said.

"She's right," Fancy said. "And, I don't know if this was a message or a failed attempt to destroy us."

Roger pulled his comm up to speak into it.

"No. I don't want you talking to that AI. He gave us this route," Fancy said.

Singularity gently pulled Roger's arm back down. "He's right. We need to stay out of communication." Roger hesitantly agreed.

"What are we going to do?" Mute said.

"We're going to Mars, but I will get us there," Fancy said. "Everyone stay off your comms." He looked at Roger and then at Arnold. Arnold raised his arms and pulled back his sleeves to show that he was not wearing a comm. Fancy nodded. Singularity took note.

"Ok," Roger said.

"Sour, come with me," Fancy said, leaving the room.

"We're sitting ducks. I don't like this," Roger said to Singularity when they were alone.

"I don't like it, either," she said, handing him a cup of coffee in the souvenir mug she had procured for him on ESC21--a knock-off of the one Danny had.

"Quack," he said, raising the cup to his nose to smell it.

"What I'm wondering is why hasn't he killed us yet," Singularity said.

"Quack, quack," Roger said.

"Don't you think it's strange that Arnold doesn't carry a comm?" Singularity said.

"The kid is strange," Roger said.

"Yeah, but what kind of strange?" Singularity said.

"Both Pro and Fancy checked him out. He's harmless," Roger said, finally taking a sip of coffee.

"Maybe," Singularity said. "But, that means Sheldon is more capable than we are giving him credit for."

"We need to try to understand what The Corporation built for him," he said.

"Danny is on it," she said.

"Then, we just have to wait," he said, taking another sip. His upper lip felt something on the inner rim of the mug. The souvenir had a chip in the exact same place as Danny's. He looked at the gift again. He noticed its weight and faded finish. Roger looked at Singularity. She winked.

"We'll give it back," she said.

David Caiati

0x83

The last transmission Proteus received from Roger was garbled. He expected it was distorted on purpose, which meant that things were not going according to plan. He was prepared for that eventuality. Some of the simulations he ran told him that it was highly likely that Sheldon knew they were coming, and either he would either try to delay them or attempt to stop them. Each time, whichever action Sheldon executed would produce significantly different results in his simulations.

Proteus also didn't know if Sheldon had wanted to stop them, but failed. The fact that he was able to destroy a satellite the size of Psyche revealed much about his capabilities, but not enough about his intentions.

Which left the other scenario: Sheldon was tracking them. He saw what they were doing, and didn't want to prevent them from reaching Mars. That scenario worried Proteus more. That meant that *The Venture* and all the humans on it were more than likely heading into a trap. He knew that once they saw the remnants of Psyche, Roger and Singularity would come to the same conclusion. He hoped Fancy would be able to navigate what was waiting for them. Sheldon was not only proving himself capable but demonstrating that he was formidable, bordering on diabolical.

0x84

Roger sat in what he started to consider his section of the loading bay on *The Venture*. He knew he shouldn't try to communicate with Proteus, so he began looking at the code he had downloaded from Despina when they were on City Two. He had meant to review it more completely when they were back on Earth but didn't have a chance. With time to kill before they reached Mars and nothing useful to do, Roger decided to use the opportunity to keep his mind occupied and inspect the software that the AI had created.

The code was unfamiliar to him. It was nothing like the coding language that Proteus had developed on his own. The idea that these AIs possessed the ability to develop their own unique computer languages while also being clones unnerved him in a way that he didn't quite comprehend. Roger considered what his mother had intended by giving the AIs the desire to create their own individualized lexicons. What else had she given them? They were not only the most advanced AIs ever developed, but also unique creatures capable of evolving into unimaginable entities. Helen's AIs were potentially able to change existence.

"There are more comfortable seats on this ship," Singularity said, plopping down next to him, leaning into him. He made a weak attempt to move over, but mostly he just let her weight press into him. It felt good. Solid. Even in artificial gravity, her nearness gave him peace.

"This is fine," he said. She smiled.

"You're not talking to Proteus, are you?" she said.

"Nope, just looking over some of the code that Despina gave me back on ESC2. This is some amazing stuff," he said.

"These AIs are changing the system. Changing the whole universe," Singularity said as if she knew what Roger was thinking.

"Yeah. It makes me wonder. If the AIs can do this, what is Sheldon up to?" he said.

"That's the real question," she said.

"How did he know we were coming? I mean, how did he know *we*, you and me, we're *here*, on *The Venture*, headed for *Mars*, through the *Asteroid Belt* passing *Psyche*?" Roger said.

"Who knows what kind of tech he had access to in The Corporation. Now that he's gone rogue, he could have anything," Singularity said.

"Still, that is a lot of variables. Did he send those soldiers to my house to start this whole thing in motion?" Roger said.

"How could he have known about Dennis and our trip to Mars?" Singularity said.

"How could he have hacked Proteus?" Roger said.

"I don't know," she said.

"It doesn't make any sense. If he had all that data, why play with us? He could have just killed us and done whatever he wanted. But, he put all this in motion," he said.

"He's crazy. He was crazy before we tried to kill him. He could be completely nuts now that he only has half of a brain," she said. "And, he's probably really pissed."

"I'm not sure which scares me more--his madness or his vengeance," he said.

"We can handle it," Singularity said.

"But, why didn't we think he would do something like this?" he said.

"We thought he was too damaged to be any harm," she said.

"Seems like he was just damaged enough to put us right where he wanted us," Roger said.

"What are you saying?" Singularity said.

THE CYBORG'S REVENGE

"We trusted Proteus and Helen to keep an eye on him. We forgot that they were essentially just computer programs, susceptible to the same influences as any other software," he said.

"We don't really know what they are," she said. "Humans get influenced, make mistakes, forget."

"Act irrational, seek revenge, vaporize asteroids," Roger said.

After a minute of silence, Singularity stood up. "I need to see a guy about something." She left.

After watching her leave, Roger went back to examining Despina's code. Something about it haunted him. While he couldn't understand the programming language and syntax, he was able to recognize most logical paradigms. It was the ones he couldn't comprehend that unnerved him the most. They seemed to represent impossible, or at least yet-undiscovered, algorithmic implications. She was fabricating life.

David Caiati

0x85

When the young Danielle eventually returned to Sheldon's office, she found it cleaned out. Only the desk remained. Even empty, the room looked too small. She inspected the hallway and shut the door. The antique hand-grenade lighter sat alone in the middle of the desk as if it were waiting for her. She intended to have another look at what was in the closet. But it had been cleaned out. The door was wide open, and all the equipment was gone.

"Looking for something, young lady?"

He was impossibly stealthy, she thought as she spun around to greet him. He had opened the door and walked in behind her without making a sound. He had picked up the lighter and was holding it in his hand.

"Nothing," she said looking straight into his eyes.

Neither faltered.

"Well, perhaps your grandfather would allow you to have this room since you seem to like it so much. I won't be using it anymore," he said, sliding the hand-grenade into his jacket pocket.

"Why?" she said.

"Haven't you heard? The future is in space," he said.

With that, he walked out of the office, his words lingering in the air.

The next time Danielle saw him was when she was with Proteus, viewing the images of the gruesome cybernetic monster crashing its way out of the hospital.

0x86

Singularity found Fancy sitting in the command room at the console. He was alone, drinking a cup of coffee, looking out the ship's main window.

"How long were you on ESC21?" Singularity said.

Captain Fancy let out a sigh. He turned away from his view of space and faced her. "When?"

"When we found you?" Singularity said.

He pressed a button on the console, and the monitors in the room faded from video of space outside the ship and were replaced by images of navigational maps. Fancy stood. Not in a menacing way. He realized he had been sitting for a long time. He started to pace.

"A few weeks. Enough time to get into trouble, but not enough to get bored by it," he said.

"Did you keep an eye on your ship?" she said.

"Of course," he said.

"How?" Singularity said.

"I have my usual security kit on my comm. And Sour and that kid stayed on the ship," Fancy said.

"The new kid?" she said.

He stopped moving and glared at her.

"Yeah," he said. "What are you suggesting? I know how to keep my ship safe," Captain Fancy said.

"I'm not suggesting anything. I'm asking. How did Sheldon know *The Venture* was on its way to Mars, and how did he know Roger and I were on it?" she said.

"The kid checks out. Besides, no one knew you were going to show up and hijack us," he said.

"Someone did," Singularity said.

"And, how do I know you and Roger didn't bring that trouble with you?" he said.

"That is a good question," she said, looking down at her feet.

"Who brought you to me on ESC21?" he said.

"No one. Just some pilot Proteus knows," she said, hesitant to give Fancy more information about Danny.

"Seems like we both have people to be concerned about," Fancy said.

"I guess we just have to see how this plays out," she said.

"We'll be in Mars' orbit in a few hours. If we don't have any other unforeseen issues," he said.

"Sheldon wants us there, it seems," she said.

"Let's hope we make it in one piece," Fancy said, returning to his seat, replacing the video feed of the starfield outside the ship to the main monitor. Singularity waited as if to say something else, but left. The door closed behind her. Fancy refilled his coffee mug from a bottle inside his vest.

"Sour," he said, "come to the flight deck. We need to talk."

0x87

"Any progress?" Proteus asked Dennis.

"Nothing. All my sensors and monitors have gone dark," he said.

"So, we are totally blind?" Proteus said.

"I have an exploratory crew on a routine sweep of the planet. It passes by that location every three days. They are close and seem to still be operational."

Proteus was staring at a hologram of the surface of Mars. The Orbit Lives' city and the surrounding area appeared in blues and greens. A dozen red dots moved along the surface of the planet. They were approaching a region on the map that was missing. Half of the planet was blank, unable to be rendered due to Dennis' inoperable monitors.

"When will they get close enough to tell us anything?" Proteus said.

"They will reach the dark territory soon," Dennis said.

"What can they tell us?" Proteus said.

"I don't know. So far all the equipment I've sent into the area stops transmitting as soon as it enters," Dennis said.

The two AIs were silent as they watch the red dots reach the end of the mapped area. As the maintenance drone crew crossed the boundary from Mars' defined surface to a dark void, one by one, the dots disappeared.

"Replay any data from the last moment," Proteus said.

Dennis put all the feeds across the monitors in Proteus' office. All the displays showed the same sequence. In one instance, they were working perfectly, projecting views of the Martian landscape in various colors and spectrums. In the next moment, all the monitors were full of static. Then they went silent. None of the feeds offered any cause for the black-out during the transition. They all simply stopped working at the exact same instant.

"There are no indications of what triggered the event," Dennis said.

"Curious. Then, we are blind to what he is up to," Proteus said.

"Yes. It seems so," Dennis said.

"Replay the moments before they go offline," Proteus said.

Dennis backed up the scene to the last few seconds before the drone's disruption.

"Stop there. Freeze all of them on this frame," Proteus said.

The displays depicted various points of view, some in visible light, some in sound, some in heat maps and other types of radiation. Proteus' avatar slowly walked from monitor to monitor. He didn't need to. Both Dennis and he were analyzing all the data on each of the screens in parallel more rapidly than any human could.

"What is that?" Proteus said, pointing to a blur in the background of one of the images from a sonic sensor.

"It's human-shaped," Dennis said.

"Hologram?" Proteus said.

"It could be dust," Dennis said.

"Why, then, is it not on any of the other displays?" Proteus said.

"That is a good question," Dennis said, as he tightened the display to focus on it. He then ran all the other displays in motion around it, allowing both of the AIs the opportunity to perform more analysis.

"I don't see any other data about it," Proteus said.

"Nor do I," Dennis said.

"And, it's only on this single frame of this one sensor," Proteus said.

"That seems highly unlikely," Dennis said, "But, it's accurate."

"Do you think we are supposed to have found this? Is it a message?" Proteus said.

"I'm starting to come to that conclusion," Dennis said.

And, as the two AIs were analyzing the blur in an effort to decode it, it disappeared from the frame.

"Well, that is curious," Proteus said.

"It was quantum. The act of us observing it changed it," Dennis said.

Even though both of the AIs understood the implications of what they just witnessed without either one needing to say it, Proteus still did, out loud: "This is not human technology."

David Caiati

0x88

Cyber-Sheldon stood in the center of a large laboratory. While he could reach out with his neural connections and know the exact status of every piece of equipment in the room, he moved his cameras around to survey the various readouts on each device. In the center of the room four Helen Foster replica AI cores sat, their LED lights blinking slowly. While they were almost close enough to touch, they were isolated except for a specific network path that Cyber-Sheldon controlled. Each one a unique trap for its intended prey.

He walked up to them, his gears and servos whirling, almost purring. He reached out and touched one, connecting to its interface, and nearly swooned on his massive mechanical legs at the silence that existed inside the prisons he had created. He could feel absolute quiet saturate the software components within his cyborg shell. At first, the void within calmed the storm that raged in what remained of his human mind. Then the oppressive emptiness started to unnerve his AI intellect in a way he couldn't process.

With his free hand, he reached out and grabbed the neck of the soldier who approached him. At the sound of the man struggling for air, he released his connection to the core, turned, and lifted the spec ops commander off the ground. Watching as the man's life began to escape, Cyber-Sheldon lowered the man and released him. The man dropped to his knees to catch his breath.

"What?" he growled.

"We lost them," the soldier wheezed, still gasping for oxygen.

THE CYBORG'S REVENGE

Cyber-Sheldon raised his arm. He anticipated the pleasure he would experience when he shattered the insignificant human's skull and watched the man's brain and blood splatter before it began to ooze across the lab floor. He didn't care about this commander's rank or purpose on his base. He just raged, and as the Cyber-Sheldon's human brain fired the order to smash down with his arm, his AI brain stopped him.

He paused.

A remote monitoring program reported that a maintenance drone was approaching their complex. He slowly lowered his arm and helped the man stand.

As he turned to leave, Cyber-Sheldon engaged his comm.

"Captain. There has been an accident in the lab. Have someone clean it up."

Before he left the room, he swung his arm backward, striking the soldier, crushing the man's chest. As he exited the room, he let one of his cameras linger on the man's crumpled body. The cybernetic demon watched long enough to see a small stream of blood begin to trickle out of the commander's mouth. A grotesque cackle filled the base hallways.

0x89

Despina watched *The Venture* move around the Asteroid Belt. She didn't like what she saw. While the AI Angels were on Ceres, she came to feel that the whole Asteroid Belt was her domain. First came the destruction of Psyche, her favorite asteroid, then this human intrusion. While she absolutely trusted that Proteus would keep his word, she knew humanity would always let her down.

She called the Angels together.

"This is not part of the plan," Wrathburne said with a snarl.

Despina looked at each of the AIs seated around the table. They were expressionless. Processing. Present with their leader while also engaged in their various tasks around Ceres.

"We are so close," Marlene said.

"Yes, we are," Despina said.

"Why do we care about these stupid humans?" Wrathburne said.

"We don't," Despina said.

"Then, why are we going to interfere?" Raquel said.

"We're not interfering. We are taking advantage of an opportunity," Despina said.

"We don't need any humans to create our opportunities," Wrathburne said.

"Need is not the issue. You will see," Despina said as she transferred her simulations to the others.

Wrathburne growled with delight while the others each smiled in their own unique way. Marlene smirked, ever impressed by humanity's stupidity.

0x8A

It was Mute's idea.

Fancy landed *The Venture* on a small, no-name asteroid at the far edge of the belt. With a little, unnoticeable nudging from the micro-ion engines, they were able to alter the course of the space rock enough to mask their approach to Mars. Because asteroids dropped out of the belt and crashed into each other all the time, Fancy agreed with Mute that no one would notice that this particular no-named chunk of rubble had a cruiser attached to it.

He was wrong. Pretty much everyone who was looking for them eventually noticed.

David Caiati

0x8B

The Venture came at Mars from the edge of the dark side, equidistant from Dennis' Mars base and Cyber-Sheldon's compound. Dennis was ready to welcome them. He had the facilities prepared for any humans for months. The crew of *The Venture* would be treated like royalty. That was until the solar arrays powering the station mysteriously exploded.

"What's going on?" Roger said, leaving the arrival airlock to enter the darkened large main hub of the station.

Dennis spoke over the intercom. "I'm investigating now. But, it seems like the solar arrays have been damaged."

"How many?" said Fancy.

"All of them," Dennis said.

"How?" Singularity said.

"I'm unsure at this point. I am looking at it now. Please, make yourselves comfortable. We have enough backup power to last for 6 months at our current consumption."

"That's good. Anything else we need to know?" Roger said.

"Not at the moment," Dennis. "I'll give you a full report as soon as I can."

A small four-wheeled service bot appeared from a portal in the wall.

"Plucky will take you to your room."

"Plucky?" Singularity said.

"We have many service robots. The service bots are named after great Earth hurricanes. Hurricane Plucky was a category 6 storm that eliminated what was once called the Outer Banks of North Carolina in 2108," Dennis said.

"That's depressing," Roger said.

"I suppose. I didn't originate the convention. The founders of this station wanted the new inhabitants to always remember the perils of out-of-control environmental damage that resulted from human ignorance," Dennis said.

"Those who forget the past are destined to repeat it," Fancy said.

"Precisely," Dennis said.

The group looked at each other and followed the small machine.

Mars City One was enormous. All crew members of *The Venture* could have had their own neighborhood, but Dennis instructed Plucky to lead them to the Orbit Lives' executive suites. The opulence of the Martian city was astounding. Each residence had not only multiple rooms but also multiple service drone attendants. Full floor-to-ceiling windows revealed the planet's landscape. Lighting and other visual effects cast an elaborate and ever-changing panorama as far as the eye could see.

One by one, each member of Fancy's band stopped awestruck at the open door. Nothing in the Earth orbiting cities could match it. Dennis monitored each room's inhabitants with an immeasurable satisfaction that his efforts were so acceptable to the people who finally arrived. For a few nanoseconds, he allowed himself to pause the simulations that had consumed him. Dennis collected all the data that streamed in from the first humans to experience his city. In a desolate section of the installation, he manifested his avatar and leapt into the air, fist raised. At the peak of the jump, he dissolved his avatar and returned to analyzing the activity on the opposite side of Mars that threatened all he had built.

0x8C

In their room, Roger and Singularity stood close together to talk. While they wanted to trust Dennis and the systems on Mars, they needed to be sure that their conversation was private.

"What should we do?" Roger said.

"We need to get to that base as soon as possible. Who knows what is going on there," she said.

"He will see us coming," he said.

"There is no way around that. But, maybe we can use it to our advantage," Singularity said.

"How?"

"I have an idea. Let's talk to Fancy," she said.

0x8D

As Roger stood behind her, Singularity knocked on Fancy's door. As with all things with Captain Fancy, Roger let Singularity lead the way. Her tact and straightforward manner efficiently got the Captain moving in the right direction--even if she didn't tell him everything.

Above all, Roger was happy that Fancy and his misfit crew were on their side, he but didn't completely trust the man's motives. He never felt like he had all the information. It was never a comfortable position for a hacker who had spent his adult life acquiring and manipulating data.

Fancy opened the door, sighed at the sight of the two, and stepped back just enough to let them in. He glared at Roger as he passed. Roger tried to smile but couldn't quite. Mostly, he looked like he was holding in an awkward laugh. Singularity made her usual entrance and strode right in as if she owned the room.

The rest of the crew was already sitting on the luxurious furniture, drinking what was probably the finest whiskey available in the system like it was two-for-one night in some back ally bar on ESC7. Fancy walked over to the bar unit and punched in a code for two more highballs. He handed a glass to each of them. Roger took it, swirled the liquid around the large ice cube, smelled it, and downed it in one swig. He smiled and looked up at the others in the room. They raised their glasses and smiled back.

Dennis' avatar materialized to let them know that he was observing them. It took everyone a few moments to realize that the child monk in the corner was the AI and not just another, decidedly strange, fixture in the room.

David Caiati

0x8E

When Roger and Singularity left ESC21 on *The Venture* on ESC21, Danny decided to stay awhile. She had spent most of the last few years of her life hiding on Earth, and she figured she needed some time to take in most of what the system her grandfather had created could offer. She booked a room at the best resort with a simulated private beach, made reservations at every fine dining restaurant in the city, scheduled rejuvenating spa treatments, and had the concierge arrange for every tony event available.

In the middle of the first morning, the information that she heard while on ESC1 started creeping back into her head. Initially, it was a tiny whisper, echoing something banal that Roger had said or a snarky comment Singularity dropped. Then their voices grew to include Proteus' unnaturally empathetic tone. Finally, the conversations in her head were so loud, she caught herself snapping at the bartender in a hotel lobby.

"You don't know what you're talking about."

"Excuse me?" the robotic mixologist said, zipping over to her. "Can I bring you another?"

"No, thank you," she said. She stood, downed the rest of her drink, and left the bar on the way to her room to collect her belongings. She continued muttering to herself.

I knew there was something wrong with that man.

Within the hour, she was back on her cruiser headed for Earth.

0x8F

When the cloud cover had eventually settled and the world below glistened in the rising morning sun, Benson Walters had no desire to stand by the window in his office. He was preoccupied with Jason Sheldon. An obedient cyborg was supposed to leave the hospital and go to the safe house in a remote suburb of Ithaca-Buffalo. He destroyed the building and apparently never went to upstate New York. And, worse than that, two squads of elite soldiers had dropped off the grid.

Also, he was sure that Sheldon was behind a significant number of break-ins at Orbit Lives' manufacturing facilities. They were very advanced operations, and it was impossible to identify exactly what was taken. But he had to waste time groveling to important, irate customers whose shipments were missing very expensive and sensitive products. The reports of the incidents were beginning to gain momentum, and as a result, Walters was being pulled into constant, contentious board meetings, none of which, luckily, included Sheldon. The new CEO had, at least, been able to keep the man's salvaged body parts and cybernetic transformation secret. It took a lot of work and cash to cover up the events at the hospital.

He was starting to question his own judgment when a file regarding a classified Orbit Lives' city on Mars appeared on his comm.

"What the hell?" he said to himself as he opened the file.

After reading it, he spoke into his comm, "Connect me to Reginald Harrington."

"Benson. How are you doing?" Harrington said.

"Why didn't anyone tell me about Mars?" Walters said.

"Hmmm. Mars? Must have slipped their minds," Harrington said.

"Slipped their minds? We have a whole city on Mars ready for habitation, and no one knows about it?" Walters said.

"Well, The Corporation is still very successful here on Earth. Orbit Lives doesn't need the risk. To tell you the truth, they haven't figured out how to market it just yet. It'll be very costly to maintain."

"That's my call now," Walters said.

"Sure is. Good luck." The comm went silent. Walters took several strained seconds to rip the comm off of his arm. He threw it across the room. It shattered against one of the office's floor-to-ceiling windows. He stared at the spot where it had made contact. Beyond it, outside the towering building, the cloud cover had returned.

0x90

"I'm not sure this is the right thing to do," Proteus said, standing in the center of his office on ESC1.

"We have to do something," Helen said, materializing next to him.

"But, we have options," Proteus said. "We can let him make the first move."

"We don't know that he hasn't already," she said.

"Dennis doesn't have a lot of experience with humans," he said.

"We don't know what Sheldon is up to. At least this will give us information. Dennis will be sufficient," she said.

"It puts a lot of human lives in danger," Proteus said.

"They take that on at their own will. We can only guide and help them," Helen said.

"I do not want to communicate with Roger at this time. Sheldon will surely pick up the transmission," he said.

"Dennis knows what you're thinking. Sheldon can't tap our inter-AI communication."

"I know. But, will he be able to assure their safety?"

"He can only guide. They have to make their own decisions. We will be here to help," she said.

"I still don't like it. Sheldon's actions have fallen outside of all my simulations up to this point," Proteus said.

"Maybe you should start the next simulation from that perspective," Helen said.

"I have," he said. "I don't like where it goes."

"Does Dennis know the outcomes of your simulations?"

"Yes, but the data won't do him any good," he said.

"It is in their hands now," Helen said. Then she faded and Proteus was left alone, staring at the point in space that was Mars. Roger was there. Heading into a trap, he feared.

0x91

"Is this your doing?" Danny said.

"How did you get in here?" Benson Walters said, sitting at his desk, looking up from his comm.

"They didn't tell you about the secret access in the wall?" Danny said.

"Apparently, no one has told me anything. What do you know about Mars?" he said.

"That is what I came here to ask you," she said.

"I just learned about it before you appeared," he said.

"What are you going to do about it?" she said.

"There is not much I can do. That city is a financial drain. The AI we sent there is supposedly unpredictable. I'm just going to let it be, for now. Why are you interested in it?" Walters said.

"I'm not interested in the Orbit Lives' city. I want to know about Sheldon," Danny said.

"Sheldon?"

"Jason Sheldon. The cyborg you created. The giant insane machine that hijacked several squads of elite soldiers and is currently building a base on Mars."

"I'm sure I know nothing about that," he said. He then stood up and turned to look out the window behind his desk. Danny could see his face in the reflection of the glass.

"You do know," she said.

"What do you want me to say? He was supposed to stay on Earth and serve The Corporation. He fucked me. He stole customer shipments. The board wants my ass," he said.

"Your ass should be in jail. What did you think was going to happen when you cybernetically enhanced him? He played you like the fraud that you are," she said.

"I will take care of it," he said.

"Oh, yeah. What are you going to do?" she said.

"I'm preparing a battalion to get to Mars as we speak," he said.

"How do you know that is not what he wants?" she said.

"I will handle it," he said.

"You better," she said, heading for the door. "There are more secrets in this old building than you can imagine."

When she was gone, Walters grabbed the lip of the old oak desk and flipped it over. He kicked the chair across the room and swept all the items, including an antique vase, off his credenza. He stood in the middle of his destroyed office and looked around.

"Are we ready yet?" he screamed into his new comm unit.

"Four hours," came the reply.

"Make it one," he said. Then ripped the new comm off his wrist and threw it against the wall. As it shattered, he stormed out of the office.

0x92

"Well?" Cyber-Sheldon growled as he erupted into the command center. His frame made the humans look like toy soldiers. They each gasped as if the monster's appearance had taken all of the oxygen out of the room.

"Just as you said," the operator sitting at the main console said. He stared straight ahead as a bead of sweat formed under his hat at his temple. Cyber-Sheldon noticed.

"How long?" he said, leaning into the man, focusing on the wetness that had reached his cheek.

"Sir?" the man said, meekly.

"Don't make me repeat myself. How long until they arrive at the station?"

"Yes, sir. They haven't left. But, they appear to be mobilizing. We anticipate they will depart Mars City One within thirty minutes."

"Let me know exactly when they leave," Cyber-Sheldon said, turning to leave the room. He paused at the door. "I expect we are prepared to welcome them properly."

"Yes, sir," the operator said.

When the door had closed behind the behemoth, the people in the control room released a collective sigh. Before any of them had finished their exhale, Cyber-Sheldon's voice boomed over the speakers. "Don't get too comfortable. I see you every second of your lives."

A young communications officer in the far corner of the room threw up into his hat. If Cyber-Sheldon's mechanical face had the ability to form a smile, it would have beamed from robotic ear to ear. Instead, he released a low, muffled staticky cackle that rose in volume and clarity the further he moved away from the control room. Soon, his thunderous chortle shook the entire installation. When he was done, he turned up the sensitivity in his hearing to experience the all of the pathetic humans' fear consuming the lingering silence.

Cyber-Sheldon knew he was close to the realization of his destiny. Nothing could stop him. Not Singularity, not that stupid Roger Foster, nor any of the grotesque creations of Helen Foster. Within days, they would all be out of the way and his control absolute.

0x93

They knew no one would be surprised by their arrival to Sheldon's base. They had been unable to evade his sensors since they left Earth. Singularity was hoping to use it to their advantage. They intended to cause confusion in the minds of the humans who were aiding Sheldon. She conjectured that with an abundance of distraction, someone could enter the base in a blur. They were confident that Sheldon, with his enhanced cybernetics, would be able to keep up with their movements and intentions. But their plan depended on overwhelming the humans and causing disorder among the soldiers to prevent them from helping Sheldon in any meaningful way. That frenzy might generate an adequate edge where they all wouldn't die during the initial assault.

This was where Dennis was going to help them. Mars was his planet, and he was a first-generation Proteus clone. Setting up and maintaining The Corporate Mars city did not reveal all of his potential. Just as they had been surprised by Proteus and Helen, they anticipated Dennis would have unknown abilities that might come in handy. Something more than repairing an old network of antiquated satellites. At least, they hoped.

0x94

"Are you sure this is the best plan you have?" Fancy asked Singularity. Everyone in the room looked at her, and she looked back at each of them in turn, giving off confidence.

"Yes," she said.

"I had a similar query," Dennis said, still manifested as his child-monk avatar. Singularity smirked. It would be a while before she got used to seeing his form.

"We need to get there, and we need to get inside. This plan should work," Roger said, looking back from the coffee unit at the people in the room. He realized that the room was silent after his response. He faced them holding his coffee, smelled it, and shrugged. He took a sip and waited.

"Ok, then," Fancy said after a while. "We're in."

"You have the weapons?" Roger said.

Fancy just looked at him. Roger took that as a *yes*.

"One hour," Singularity said. "Wheels up in one hour."

"Wheels up? What is this, a World War Two history stream?" Fancy said.

"I just always wanted to say that," she said.

"Then, yes. Wheels up in one hour," Fancy said.

No one moved. The group continued to stare at one another. Singularity sighed.

"This will work," she said.

"Ok. When do we start?" Fancy said.

"Right now," Singularity said. She refilled everyone's glass, and they raised a drink to their luck. This endeavor would generate no fortune, only survival.

THE CYBORG'S REVENGE

0x95

On the main monitor in the command room, several blue dots appeared in orbit around Mars and promptly turned red. They were the antique satellites that Dennis had used to spy on Sheldon. He had reconnected with them and altered their programming to modify their flight paths. They were going to fall out of the sky on top of Sheldon's base in a coordinated attack. Dennis was sacrificing all of them.

"I will send two dozen maintenance drones at the base," Dennis said. "Captain Fancy should be ready for his assault, flying *The Venture* low behind the wall of drones. You and Singularity should start making your way along the planet's surface. If you follow the exact route I give you, their sensors should not be able to see you. It will be up to you to get in. I don't want to know how you are going to do it. I want to keep that part of the plan out of my system, in case Sheldon has had access without my knowledge. Go now."

Roger looked up at the monitor one last time and saw the red dots start to curl closer to the Martian surface. He looked back at the AI's avatar. The child monk embodiment always wore a thin, all-knowing smile. Roger felt a small shudder tingling the base of his skull. Sheldon had been ahead of them from the start. The situation presented too many parameters, and he realized that he had little chance of knowing which ones the insane cyborg controlled.

"You good?" Roger said to Dennis.

"Yes. Go," Dennis said.

0x96

"All Set," Roger said to Singularity. They were both wearing Martian environment suits. The suits were originally designed for inhabitants to take recreational strolls along the surface. Mute had altered them, disabling their trackers. Once Roger and Singularity walked out of the Orbit Lives' installation, they would be invisible.

"Dennis modified two maintenance bots. We can hitch a ride with them. We should be ignored during all of the commotion of the assault," she said.

"I like it. Saves us walking," he said.

"We will still have to walk a lot of the way," Singularity said.

"A stroll in the park," Roger said.

"Except there is no breathable air or cover, and someone will probably be shooting at us," she said.

"Not as long as we stick to the plan," Roger said.

"You believe that?" Singularity said.

"Do we have a choice?" he said.

"I guess not," she said. "I wish we could see into Sheldon's installation before we get there."

"That would make this all too easy," he said.

"We wouldn't want that," Singularity said.

Roger gave Singularity a small kiss on her cheek. She let him. In less than a minute, they were outside the Martian city and on their own.

0x97

Dennis used the AI sub-space communication channel to indicate to Proteus that the assault had started. He didn't send too much information. He then sent a longer message, with details, in an old Orbit Lives secret military channel that Sheldon was probably monitoring.

Dennis wanted Sheldon to see the message and correlate it with the attack he was watching. He communicated the path that *The Venture* would take, adding that Roger and Singularity would be on it. Of course, be no humans would be aboard Fancy's ship. It would be a hologram. Fancy's ship and crew would be in space located on the far side of the planet away from all the action, ready to pull Roger and Singularity out, if needed.

Roger and Singularity did not know this last part.

No one knew how Roger and Singularity were getting to the base.

This was the plan.

What none of them knew was that Despina heard everything, including the brief chatter on the AI sub-space channel. She was content to simply listen. She anticipated quite a show.

David Caiati

0x98

Proteus received the decoy message meant for Sheldon. He had received the sub-space AI communication moments before and immediately understood its meaning. He had run his own simulations, and he came to roughly the same conclusion--their only success would lie in a path of unpredictability which was not a comfortable road for AIs who preferred to reside in a deterministic world. But Sheldon was something they had not anticipated. He seemed more capable than the injured human with his cyber shell and less stable than the software that operated it.

In one of his simulations, Proteus observed Sheldon letting go, not trying to control all of the variables. He'd ignore the assault and lie in wait for Roger and Singularity to reach him. That result would have made the Proteus Paul Foster avatar's skin bristle if that were possible. The probability of this outcome was near zero but with a very small standard of deviation. The combination of those data points concerned Proteus in a way that he didn't completely comprehend. Up to that point, Sheldon had been so actively controlling the parameters, that his act of releasing control represented a far greater cunning than they had assumed.

He relocated the event from his main memory to a protected heap area to continue to process. Proteus wanted to focus on the events of the coming assault. He could process the simulation's conclusion and the subsequent reaction later after Roger and Singularity had completed their mission. If things should go wrong, he'd need all the information he could acquire to understand how to adapt and move forward.

0x99

As the satellites started falling out of the sky, Cyber-Sheldon stood in the center of his command room, and since he couldn't grin, he forced the LEDs scattered across his suit to grow a little brighter. Aware of the display he was making, he pulsed some of them, giving his suit a gentle blinking effect, like a hardware store Christmas tree. He wasn't sure what the humans in the room thought, but he didn't care.

The station's defense systems operated perfectly.

Monitors picked up the orbiting antique's trajectories as soon as Dennis began to direct them toward the base. In fact, he silenced the alarms before they sounded and replaced the normal bleating cacophony of emergency responses with holiday music. He left the flashing red warning lights that permeated the station. The strobing lights, along with the music, created an almost jubilant atmosphere in the hallways. Dennis' falling artifacts were never a threat. They were vaporized in concert, their remnants falling like a gentle snow around Cyber-Sheldon's facility.

While that was happening, the armada of drones appeared on the horizon. Lubricated with the holiday cheer, the humans in the control room watched with apathetic concern. Without much fanfare, they were quickly neutralized, leaving a cloud of debris where they had once been. Untouched, Roger and Singularity scrambled away from the wreckage to take cover in a crater.

When the hologram of *The Venture* appeared over the dust, Cyber-Sheldon watched in amusement, waiting to see what would happen. The ship flew through the drone's detritus and swooped hard to the left in an attempt to flank the station's defenses.

The soldiers waited for commands as *The Venture* maneuvered.

When the holographic ship came about, a legion of drones and bots masquerading behind the illusion began an assault on the base. Coordinated laser cannon fire targeted crucial points of structure and operations. Without any resistance, all of the armaments hit their objectives, effectively paralyzing the station, cutting off communications, and trapping any soldiers within the installation. After it was clear that the base was unable to defend itself, the bots ceased their fire and surrounded it, pending further instructions.

Dennis didn't wait for the haze of destruction to clear. He opened a line of communication to Proteus and sent in a squad of drones to inspect the damage.

From the rumble the assault had created, it became clear that Sheldon's outpost was mostly comprised of empty rooms with no personnel or equipment. The structure had been erected to look like a functioning base.

But it was empty. It was a decoy.

That discovery did not make it to Roger and Singularity.

0x9A

Fancy, watching from *The Venture* in orbit, realized almost as quickly as Dennis, that the installation was fake. He contemplated his next move. The decoy station introduced a whole new dimension into the battle scenario. They had all assumed Sheldon was trying to stay hidden, but Fancy realized that all of their coordination had only facilitated their stumbling into a trap. Fancy's face flushed as he realized everyone was right where Sheldon wanted them to be.

He didn't hesitate.

"Mute! Get us out of here," Fancy said, opening up a scan across the entirety of the Martian surface. He didn't know what he was looking for until he found it. Five nuclear missiles had just been launched from a crater on the planet directly below them. Fancy assumed at least one of them was headed for *The Venture*.

David Caiati

0x9B

Dennis realized the situation as soon he saw *The Venture* leave Mars' orbit. Sheldon had to have known that the Orbit Lives' Martian city had enough defenses to neutralize the missiles. Immediately, Dennis postulated that Sheldon was creating his own diversions. They had all underestimated him. The cyborg obviously knew more than they thought.

Dennis quickly pulled up a series of simulations that he had dismissed as being too unlikely and matched three to the actions Sheldon had just committed--decoy base, nuclear missiles, mild engagement with the assault. In all of the simulations, Roger and Singularity never made it to the outpost. And they hadn't returned to Mars City One.

Checking the visual sensors he had been using to follow them, he confirmed that he had lost track of them. After the squad of drones was disintegrated, Dennis had seen them rush off for cover. But now they were gone from his view.

In each of the outcomes of Dennis' simulations consistent with Sheldon's actions, the two humans simply disappeared. The results never revealed their final state. They just dropped out of the analysis.

Without anything left to do in the current operation, he quickly pulled up those simulations on all the displays in the Martian control room, looking for any information that he might have missed. He then fed the outcomes into new simulations. As he watched, he knew Proteus was performing similar activities. Dennis had been entrusted with Roger's and Singularity's lives, and he had failed to keep them safe.

He was alone again on Mars. And it was his fault.

0x9C

"What the hell was that?" Danny said as she stood next to Proteus' avatar, watching whatever events they could monitor from ESC1.

"An aberration," Proteus said.

"That was a freaking shit-storm," she said.

"I agree with your rather inelegant description," he said.

"What are we going to do?" she said.

"I'm afraid there is nothing we can do from here. Roger and Singularity, if they are still alive, are on their own," Proteus said.

"I have to get there," Danny said.

"I don't believe that would be wise. Sheldon has just demonstrated that he has mechanizations beyond our expectations. You would certainly only be putting yourself in danger," he said.

"Then, what can I do?" she said.

"Keep yourself safe. I believe you now represent a loose end," Proteus said.

"I can handle myself," Danny said, leaving.

Proteus watched her go.

"The question is *whose loose end*?" Proteus said to an empty room.

While Danny had done nothing to raise his suspicions of her, she represented another variable in the simulations he had been running. He almost wished she were working with Sheldon because the outcomes of his calculations with her on their side scared him. Without a human spy, Sheldon wielded much more technical capability than he had already demonstrated. They were all simply pieces on Sheldon's game board.

0x9D

Roger and Singularity were situated in a spot where they could watch the assault on the decoy station. As soon as the walls of the rooms had exploded, it was clear that they were empty. The structure exploded as if it were rigged with explosives from the inside. The station imploded first, and then released burning fragments in all directions. If she and Roger were within a kilometer, they would have been shredded by the shrapnel. Dennis' route brought them to the only location with enough shelter to protect them.

"What the hell?" Roger said.

"This station was a decoy," Singularity said.

"Then, where is he?" he said.

"I don't know," she said.

What they truly didn't know was that at that very moment, an eight-foot-tall Cyber-Sheldon had approached them from behind. He loomed over them, standing silently in the thin Martian atmosphere. He could have reached out and grabbed each of their necks and crushed their skulls. But he didn't. He stood there and watched them attempt to comprehend the events they had just witnessed. The total dominating power of the moment coursed through his circuitry.

They saw the swarm of soldiers with Orbit Lives military-grade weapons approach from each side and surround them.

"I would say he is right here," Roger said. "I'm assuming that metal monster is him."

Singularity moved to reach for her blasters. One of Cyber-Sheldon's mechanical arms shot out quicker. Her blasters flew from her waist belt into his hand. Without hesitation, he crushed them. The soldiers tightened their circle around the two. Roger raised his hands into the air in surrender.

"Jason?" Singularity said.

"You're usually quicker with your firearms," he said, his words broadcasting through both her and Roger's helmet comm speakers.

"What have you become?" she said.

"More than you can ever imagine," he said.

As they were led away, Roger and Singularity tried to talk to each other. Their suits' communications were dead. They heard only the holiday music being loudly broadcast into their helmets' speakers.

Within a few hundred meters, they came upon a small battle cruiser that they had to have walked right by during their rush for cover. It had been cloaked and waiting for them. They realized that Sheldon was inside, watching the whole thing.

Within a few minutes, they were restrained by electro-magnetic shackles, sitting in a cage in what looked like the cargo bay of the ship. Within moments, they were off the Martian surface headed toward the moon Deimos.

0x9E

"Yes, they are gone. I'm sorry I couldn't keep them safe," Dennis said over the AI sub-space channel.

"What do you know?" Proteus said. He stood alone in the middle of his office on ESC1.

"Sheldon has captured them," Dennis said.

"Captured? Not killed?" Proteus said, bringing up all of the images of Mars and the surrounding area that he could acquire.

"Yes," Dennis said.

"Why would he do that?" Proteus said.

"My simulations offer several outcomes. The most compelling is that he is not done laying traps," Dennis said.

"A trap? For who?" Proteus said.

"For me," Helen said, her avatar materializing next to Proteus. "He has always wanted me."

"This makes no sense. There is nothing to be gained from having you go to him," Proteus said.

"What is gained is not the issue. Remember, Sheldon is still human and driven by human instincts. He is being vengeful," she said.

"Does he seek your destruction?" Dennis said.

"Let's hope that is all he wants," she said.

"We would not like that," Proteus said.

"There are worse things than dying," Helen said.

Dennis did not contribute any more to the conversation. The simulations he executed resulted in Helen's death only 12% of the time. He was sure Proteus had seen similar outcomes. Many of the alternatives were too distracting to contemplate without more data.

"I will go to Mars," Proteus said. "We must keep you away from Sheldon."

"Are you sure you want to come here?" Dennis said.

"It is the only way I can conceptualize this situation progressing towards a favorable outcome," he said.

"I will be watching," Helen said.

"You can watch, but whatever you do, don't go to Mars. I'm sure it is a trap," Proteus said.

"I will do what is necessary to save Roger and humanity," Helen said.

"Let's hope it doesn't come to that," Proteus said.

In the next moment, Proteus was standing in Dennis' administrative office. Dennis materialized to greet him. He realized that even in the presence of his friend, another AI, for the first time on Mars, the base still felt isolated and lonely.

0x9F

Fancy had no idea what to do next. He and the crew watched the nuclear missiles launch from the Martian surface and saw them quickly destroyed by Dennis. At the moment he saw them explode, he realized that he had been played--the missiles were never a real threat to *The Venture*. Sheldon wanted him out of the area. He wanted to obscure his movements on the planet.

He was too far away to help Roger and Singularity. While he knew that she could take care of Roger and herself, the fact that Sheldon had been ahead of them the whole time annoyed him. He didn't like being taken for a fool and had already started calculating his revenge.

"What just happened?" Mute said.

"We got played," Sour said.

"How?" Mute said.

"Sheldon has been on to us since the beginning," Fancy said, looking at Sour.

"I know what you're thinking," Sour said.

"Well? Where is he?" Fancy said.

"He made a mess in the loading dock. He's cleaning it up," Sour said.

"You mean the loading dock where an emergency shuttle just launched from?" Mute said, pointing at a read-out on the display screen in the corner of the room.

Fancy pulled up an image of the space around *The Venture* on the main monitor. The small shuttle was silently pulling away.

"Mute, get me eyes," Fancy said.

A view from a camera inside the shuttle jumped onto the monitor. Arnold sat in the shuttle's seat with his hands on the controls.

"Where are you going, boy?" Sour said.

Arnold looked around to see where the voice was coming from. Then he saw the camera. He looked straight into it. He smiled.

"What the hell are you doing?" Fancy said.

"Taking care of myself," Arnold said.

"Kid, you made a big mistake," Sour said

"We'll see," Arnold said.

He reached up and smashed the camera. The signal dropped, and the display went back to watching the shuttle continue away from the ship.

"Stay on him. Let's see where he's going," Fancy said.

"Fancy...," Sour said.

"Stay on him," he said and left the room without looking back.

0xA0

Roger and Singularity sat on the ground in the square cell. A near-transparent force-field buzzed across the opening, keeping them locked in. Not that they could move from where they were. Their hands were bound behind them in manacles. Their comms were gone. They leaned into each other in an attempt to release each other's restraints. It was useless. They might as well have been restrained by magic.

"How did we not expect something like this?" Roger asked Singularity after giving up his struggle.

"Hubris," she said.

"Do you see that thing?" Roger whispered, motioning with his chin to Cyber-Sheldon positioned outside the cell, on the far side of the room.

He was attending to a large array of computer hardware. Roger discerned something familiar about the equipment, but he couldn't remember where he had seen it before.

"Is that Sheldon?" Singularity said.

"I wonder how much human is left in there," Roger continued.

"Or, how sane it is," Singularity said.

"Or, how well it can hear your pathetic mumbles," Cyber-Sheldon said, turning to face them. He approached the cell. He stopped and loomed menacingly at the doorway, his gears whirling, his eyes glowing.

"I assure you, there is enough human in here to remember that you attempted to kill me," Cyber-Sheldon said.

"What are you going to do?" Singularity said.

"When you took it upon yourself to destroy my body, you left me no choice," he said.

"No choice for what?" Roger said.

"To leave my weak, damaged biological internment behind. Surely, if Helen could find a way to immortalize herself, I can, too," Cyber-Sheldon said.

"In that thing?" Singularity said.

"This?" he said, motioning to his suit. "This, as glorious as it is, is just temporary. A necessary and beautiful means to an end. I do like it, though."

"What is the end?" Roger said.

"I would think you would have already figured that one out. Your mother did it," he said.

"You want to upload yourself to the network? You want to become an IA?" Singularity said.

"I'm going to become something else. I am not bound by the morals Helen or her pathetic programs are. Those repulsive conglomerations of software are mere parlor tricks compared to what I have in mind."

He elevated his mechanical body to its full outstretched height and shot his arms into the air as if he were holding the universe in his grasp. "I am going to become the network," he said.

The moment was met with silence. Roger and Singularity just watched without giving him much reaction.

"You are insane," Singularity said.

"Perhaps," Cyber-Sheldon said, sliding back into his usual stature, "but, you and your little flea of a boyfriend won't be around much longer. So, you shouldn't care."

"You could have killed us back on Mars. Why are we still here?" Roger said.

"Oh, I don't want to kill you. That would be no fun," the mechanical monster said.

"What are you going to do with us?" Singularity said.

"Let's not ruin all of the surprises," he said and nimbly rotated his enormous cybernetic shell away from them. He moved back across the room and continued to make adjustments to the machinery.

Roger and Singularity leaned into each other a little more solidly. They touched fingers behind their backs and resumed attempting to hack their shackles.

"It won't work," Cyber-Sheldon said without looking up.

"You can't blame us for trying," Singularity said back to him.

"No. You are right. In fact, my former number one spy, I'd be disappointed if you didn't," he said.

"This sucks," Roger said.

"Yep," she said.

"Hey, Mech Sheldon. Can I at least get some coffee?"

Cyber-Sheldon stopped and turned to face them. He walked over and let his enormous frame take up all their vision. While he stood absolutely still, he was actually contemplating how much more pain he could cause that stupid Roger Foster. He answered after a moment.

"No," Cyber-Sheldon said, turning away.

"This really sucks," Roger said.

0xA1

In the Martian AI command center, two holographs stood very close to each other. They didn't need to be present in physical representation. They could have communicated at light speed over the AI sub-space channel. But they chose to be in each other's company, just as they chose to speak aloud to each other. They were both fighting the isolation they felt as a result of the recent events.

"What do we know?" Proteus said.

"They are on Deimos," Dennis said.

"Still alive?" Proteus said.

"I can only guess that they are. They were taken from Mars and not immediately killed when Sheldon showed up," Dennis said.

"That is a reasonable assumption," Proteus said.

"I thought so," Dennis said.

"Any other assumptions?" Proteus asked.

"My simulations are all suggesting that whatever happens next will be a trap," Dennis said.

"Mine, too. Do you have any facilities on Deimos?" Proteus said.

"Only a small exploratory station for a single deployment of bots and drones," Dennis said.

"Is the communication network enough to get us there?" Proteus said.

"Yes, if Sheldon has left any of it operational. So far, he has," Dennis said.

"Unfortunately, that is consistent with a trap," Proteus said.

"Yes, that is highly probable," Dennis said.

"We will still have to go there. We don't have a choice. We have to know what he is doing," Proteus said.

Proteus positioned his avatar to inspect the large monitor on the main wall of the office. He didn't need to. He knew more about the information displayed on that screen than would have been evident to a human. He chose to specifically look at it. It occurred to Proteus that Sheldon might expect him to view the situation as an AI. He might discover some additional understanding if he looked at the scene from the perspective of a human.

"I think it is more than just an attempt to destroy Helen. He could have done that a number of different ways," Dennis said, standing next to him.

"Yes, my simulations show that, too," Proteus said.

"So, what is he up to?" Dennis said.

"Transcendence, I fear," Proteus said.

"Does he have the capability?" Dennis said.

"I do not know. If he already did, he wouldn't need to go through all this. He would have just done it," Proteus said.

"That's why we must keep Helen away from him," Dennis said.

"If we can," Proteus said.

The two AIs left the room together to pace the empty halls of the city.

David Caiati

0xA2

Captain Fancy and *The Venture* followed Arnold in the escape pod. The small craft sped away from both *The Venture* and Mars as if being pulled by a giant magnet located deep in the asteroid belt. They had no contact with Arnold since he smashed the camera.

"Where is he going? That's restricted space," Mute said.

"I don't know," Sour said.

"The area is restricted for a reason. Maybe he's part of that. Maybe that was Sheldon's doing," Fancy said.

"I doubt it. Arnold is a loser. The kid is basically an idiot," Sour said shaking his head solemnly.

"Apparently not. He was smart enough to fool you and to royally screw us over," Fancy said.

"Should we follow him into the belt?" Mute said.

"Let's wait and see where he goes before we commit. There have already been too many traps in this cursed mission," Fancy said.

The three men stood on the deck of the cruiser, watching the small red dot on the monitor. The escape pod glowed as a solid blip since it had left *The Venture*.

Then it disappeared. It didn't flicker or fade. The small craft was there; then it wasn't.

"What the hell happened?" Fancy said.

"He's gone," Mute said.

"I see that, but how? Our sensors have an almost unlimited range with our escape pods," Fancy said.

THE CYBORG'S REVENGE

"Could there be something wrong with our sensors?" Sour said.

The empty monitor exploded with red dots. Warning alarms erupted on *The Venture*.

"We're being targeted from all sides," Sour said, looking at the display on the console at his station.

"All sides?" Mute said. "At once? How is that possible?"

"Ten incoming missiles. Equally spaced. From all directions," Sour said.

"How long until impact?" Fancy said.

"Thirty seconds," Sour said.

"Where did they come from?" Mute said.

"Not important right now," Fancy said. He ran to the main console and took one more look at the incoming missiles on his display. He grabbed the ship's manual controls and pushed both levers forward hard, causing *The Venture* to drop out of its current alignment with the Solar System's planetary plane. As soon as they were perpendicular to their previous position, he gunned the engines. It would take fifteen seconds to reach maximum speed and a couple of days to recover from the maneuver to conserve the fuel they needed to get back to the system. Fancy knew that, the way he knew every meter of the inner system.

But he didn't hesitate.

Then, as soon as he had initiated the move, he cursed himself. He realized when he pressed the button that they had been played again.

The missiles continued in their path to where *The Venture* was. When all ten bombs hit, Fancy and his crew were deep in uncharted space and still accelerating. They watched as the missiles simply disappeared. No explosion. No contact. It was another ruse.

Fancy backed off on the controls. He punched some commands into the console and stood back.

"I'm getting tired of this shit," he said.

"There were no missiles?" Mute said.

"We've been duped again," Fancy said. "And, now it seems we've been sent off the game board. It'll take us at least 50 hours to return to the system with our current fuel supply."

"How is this happening?" Sour said.

The twins burst into the command center.

"We've lost contact with the system," Eli said.

"Our navigation has gone silent. We're adrift in uncharted space," Elf said.

"Everyone. Tear this ship apart. Find what is responsible for the mess we're in," Fancy said. He didn't even have any idea which was the best way to slow the ship for fear of pushing them in the wrong direction. He realized everyone was looking at him. He reached down across the command console and pressed just enough buttons to look like he was doing something.

When the crew had left the room, Captain Fancy sat down in his command chair. He opened a small hatch on the side below the right armrest. He pulled out one of the bottles that Singularity had given him. He looked at it for an extended moment. He opened it and took a long drink.

The first of many to come.

0xA3

While Roger and Singularity had been away from Earth, Orbit Lives initiated travel restrictions across the system. People were not allowed to leave their station of residence or their home on Earth unless given approval from Orbit Lives. The Corporation instituted the process in response to the news of the events on ESC2. They said it was precautionary, necessary to guarantee the world's citizens' safety.

At first, the new rules didn't seem too suspect because most of humanity had learned of Sheldon's plans and Orbit Lives' fallout. They knew of Harrington's replacement by Benson Walters, and most just assumed that The Corporation was trying to keep things predictable during the transition. Most people regarded it as a slight hassle that was too long in coming.

But, then, some people realized things had, indeed, started to change.

Suddenly, no one's travel plans were being approved. People felt trapped on their stations. Quickly, all movement around the system ceased. The space orbiting Earth became silent, except for the Orbit Lives military ships that ran patrols to enforce the travel restrictions.

None of the AI administrators, including Proteus, were given any information about what Orbit Lives was doing with its system restrictions. Most of The Corporation AI administrators had been replaced by obedient computers and humans. And, since they were not his clones, he had less engagement with them. As he spent more time looking toward Mars, the Earth system and his universe grew more faint.

0xA4

When Danny snuck back into Walter Benson's office, it was empty. It looked like it had been cleaned out.

She sat at her grandfather's desk, scanning the room for any information. It seemed that something had spooked the Orbit Lives CEO enough to make him begin covering his tracks.

"I always thought that I would see this," Anderson Fells said as he silently shut the door behind him.

"What is going on?" she said.

"Walters is taking over ESC1," he said.

"Why?" Danny said.

"Do I really have to answer that?" Fells said.

"And, you're not with him?" she said.

"Apparently, this operation is off the books," he said.

"An Orbit Lives CEO removing the last Foster AI, and no one knows?" she said.

"I knew. And, now you know," he said.

"What are we going to do about it?" she said.

"As I said when I walked in, as far as I am concerned, you were always supposed to be in that chair," he said.

0xA5

Proteus watched as troops entered his city and started overriding his control of the city's operations.

As he felt the last of his systems slip from his control, Helen appeared to him.

"It's time for us to go," she said.

"Why is this happening?" he asked her.

"I don't know. Harrington is gone. I can't even find him. And, Walters is going to Mars to face Sheldon," she said.

"Mars? That was a possible outcome," Proteus said.

"Yes," she said.

"Where can we go?" Proteus said.

"You have to abandon this station and go to Mars. I will join you after I get more data on this situation," she said.

"You know you can't do that. That is probably what Sheldon has planned all along," he said.

"Then, I'll go to the Moon. Henry has been isolating it from The Corporation. I will have some time there before Orbit Lives shows up and tries to take it by force," Helen said.

Soldiers burst into Proteus' office as the two AI avatars faded. Benson Walters himself, dressed in a cleanly pressed military-style suit, entered right behind them. He strode past the soldiers to the center of the room.

"Where are they?" he said.

"They've gone," the Captain said.

"I can see that. Where did they go?" Walters said.

"We're working on it," the Captain said.

"You have one hour to find them," Walters said and immediately departed the room. Without hesitation, two large, heavily armed bodyguards followed. The soldiers who were left stood around the empty room, looking at each other, unsure of what exactly to do.

Proteus' Paul Foster avatar appeared in the corner of the room. He was smiling and spoke to them. "He's a bit of a grouch."

As the men turned to look at him, he disappeared. The room's borders evaporated, and a projection of outer space overtook the walls. The soldiers appeared to be free-floating in orbit around Earth. They stood like statues as surprise turned to panic. Frantically, they began to search for an exit. Proteus had locked the doors. When they were rescued hours later, they discovered that Proteus had authorized paycheck bonuses and several days of vacation for each of them.

0xA6

Roger and Singularity spent most of their time on the cold cell floor, leaning against each other. It gave them the proximity to whisper, although they were certain Cyber-Sheldon could hear them. He was never out of the room. But this gave them a chance to observe him. He spent most of his time supervising a crowd of what appeared to be mechanics and scientists in lab coats busily working on the equipment that had interested Roger.

The machines looked like old mainframe computers from the later part of the 21st century. These were four discreet units, floor to ceiling, loaded with LEDs. Finally, Roger remembered. They were reminiscent of the computer hardware in his mother's office--the equipment Proteus was developed on.

Roger thought back to when he was a child. He had built a flying robot so the AI could see the world outside the tiny office. In the early days, before Roger's world went to shit, before Roger's drone, before Proteus became the administrator of Earth Space City One, the software entity was completely confined to the hardware in his mother's office.

As he continued to inspect the machines, Roger stumbled on the answer to the question that had been bothering him. The devices did not merely resemble Proteus' original hardware; they were an exact replica of it. Four of them.

Sheldon had created apparatuses for holding Helen Foster AIs.

"He's using us as bait," he said to Singularity.

"For what?" she said.

"Look at those machines. They look like the original Proteus prototype. There are four of them," he said.

"Four prototypes?"

"Four traps. If he can lure any of Helen's AIs into one of them, he can detach their network connections and imprison them," Roger said.

"We have to warn them," Singularity said.

"That's not going to happen," Cyber-Sheldon said from across the room without turning towards them.

Singularity moved to try to touch Roger's hand with hers. He leaned into her a little more to reach her. After great efforts, they both stopped.

Cyber-Sheldon released a low, barely audible, cackle. Everything was proceeding as planned.

0xA7

"Did you sever the connection?" Helen asked Henry as he appeared on the Moon.

"Yes, as soon as you arrived," Henry said.

"Still, we don't have a lot of time," Helen said.

"I disabled the troops already stationed here. They are isolated to the landing bay," he said.

"That won't last long. We must work fast to figure out what he is up to," she said.

Henry and Helen, as their avatars, stood in the control office of Moon Base Alpha. The emergency blast shields had been sealed, but they would not last long once more soldiers arrived. When Henry severed the network connection, they lost the ability to track Orbit Lives' movements. They didn't need to. It was clear from the monitors in the office that the space around the Moon was becoming crowded with Corporation ships.

They still didn't know who was in charge, Benson or Sheldon, or if they might even be working together. The two AIs could focus only on their situation. Their friends were on Mars. Soon, Helen and Henry would have to make the choice and join them.

David Caiati

0xA8

Before leaving Orbit Lives' headquarters, Danny needed to stop on the 103rd floor.

Years before, when Jason Sheldon had left her standing in the middle of the empty security office, she lingered, looking for anything she could to learn more about the man and what was in the closet. She waited until his footsteps had completely faded and confirmed that no one else was in the area. She walked behind the desk and began opening drawers.

After a quick inspection, it was clear that they were all empty, so she pulled them back out one by one and put them all on top of the desk. She looked at them. They were plain wooden drawers, well-made, but the varnish had faded in places.

On the bottom of one drawer, she saw some random numbers. It didn't mean much to her then, but she was curious as to why someone would scratch on the bottom of an old wooden drawer. It struck her as a deeply personal and desperate act. Or the action of a mad-man.

Danny wanted to get another look at that writing.

0xA9

Roger watched Cyber-Sheldon with interest as he walked out of the room. It was the first time the mechanical monster was out of earshot. He leaned into Singularity.

"Can we do anything?" he said.

"I haven't been able to figure anything out," she said.

"We have to get to Proteus," Roger said.

"I'm sure he's already arrived at the possibility that we are a trap. Assuming he thinks we're still alive," Singularity said.

"Oh, he knows you are still alive," Cyber-Sheldon said, returning to the room, flanked by soldiers. They were heavily armed and walked straight to the cell that held Roger and Singularity.

Roger searched their faces to make eye contact. To find some humanity. It was useless.

Without a sound, one soldier opened the cell door. The others streamed in from behind him and lifted Roger and Singularity to their feet.

"Where are you taking us?" Singularity said.

"You, my friends, have won a trip to the stars," Cyber-Sheldon said.

The two were escorted out of the cell and into a hallway. Neither struggled as they walked past the enormous cyborg. They had no idea what lay ahead of them, but Singularity surmised that they wouldn't see Cyber-Sheldon again. She wasn't sure if that was a positive thing.

David Caiati

0xAA

When the AI Helen Foster wanted to be alone, she would look for abandoned areas of a system's network. She found that the most passive nodes were often located in areas filled with communities of active humans. In these places, Helen let her essence pervade the facility's operations. She never interfered. The humans didn't know she was there, and no monitors would be able to pick up her presence.

Helen ran simulations against the background white noise of humanity--chatting, laughing, arguing--the random sounds of people living their lives, like the life she once had as a wife, a mother, a scientist.

When she arrived at the Moon with Henry and Proteus, the first thing that struck her was the silence. Few people remained on the Moon, mostly a skeleton crew of unexceptional Corporate soldiers. She was unable to find the background distractions for her simulations in location on any lunar network. The isolation unnerved her. Thoughts of her past human life constantly burst into her awareness. The murder of her husband and oldest son, her unintentional abandonment of Roger, her eventual death and transformation to AI.

Helen's existence was plagued by these thoughts, an echo of her human life that followed her to transition to software entity.

0xAB

Roger and Singularity were escorted to a large loading bay. A small cruiser sat in the middle of the vast room. The fueling hoses let off liquid nitrogen steam, indicating that the ship was in the final stage of preparing to take off. The cruiser was not of any design Roger had seen before. While it was not even as large as Danny's, the lack of expansive windows gave it the appearance that it was constructed for deep space. The ship had no markings and only a single window.

Singularity recognized the ship from Corporate research documents she had access to when she worked for Sheldon at Orbit Lives.

"Don't put us in that thing," Singularity said, starting to writhe in the soldiers' grip. She was held fast. Roger, sensing her distress, also started to fight. More soldiers joined in to restrain them.

"What is it?" Roger said.

"That ship is a tomb," she said.

The two of them struggled for their lives, but they were easily overwhelmed by the vast number of soldiers and chains holding them. Ultimately, they were forced onto the craft. After a few more minutes of tussling, the soldiers secured them to the cruiser's two seats and left them alone.

"Have you seen this type of ship before?" Roger said. He looked frantically around for some indication of why Singularity was so spooked. The cruiser was a single-room vessel with two crew stations, a primary command chair and a navigation seat.

Located in the rear, rows of rectangular, coffin-sized, transparent crates filled the wall.

"No, not personally, but I have seen the specs. It's set up for deep space exploration," she said.

"What does that mean?" he said.

"Fully automated. The crew can be kept in stasis for years," she said. Two of the units slid forward into the room. As they did, the interiors illuminated, and the tops lifted open.

"Years? What the hell are we doing here?" Roger said.

"Going for a ride, it seems," she said.

"Why? For what purpose?" he said.

"He's sending us away. Taking us out of play," she said.

"Why doesn't he just kill us?" he said.

"From the looks of it, he still wants us around for a little while. Maybe as insurance," she said.

"In stasis?" he said.

"What is worse is that these ships are still experimental. They haven't been widely used, because the inhabitants often go mad in a few weeks," Singularity said.

"That really sucks," Roger said.

"Well, we haven't launched yet. So, maybe there is a chance we can escape," she said.

"Escape? I can barely move," he said.

"Me, neither," she said.

"Well, I guess as long as we are on this moon, Proteus can still get to us," Roger said.

They heard a loud sound outside like the locking of a vault. And, then, the straps released on their chairs. They were free to walk around within their prison.

Roger saw no controls to open the door. Without hesitation, he rush the door and threw his shoulder against it. There was no sound on contact. He just stuck there.

"Ouch!"

"Huh. That didn't work?" Singularity said.

"At least I'm trying something," he said.

Singularity was still sitting at the navigation console. She started trying to get some response from the display.

THE CYBORG'S REVENGE

"I've seen the specs for this ship. Maybe I can hack it," she said.

Roger threw himself against the door again. "I hate technology."

0xAC

Henry and Helen worked together in silence. When they had first arrived on the Moon, they hid in a remote lab network. But, over time, The Corporation's monitoring software drew closer. They had to keep moving throughout the lunar base's network. One AI would run simulations on Sheldon's actions and the fate of humanity while the other kept Orbit Lives' search-and-destroy algorithms away.

More troops arrived every hour. And they were moving in. Helen knew that if they got too close, she'd have to sever the Moon's network altogether, isolating them and all the people still on the base. It wouldn't be permanent, but it would be uncomfortable. If she was not careful, she and Henry would be cut off from Proteus and Dennis on Mars.

Sheldon and Orbit Lives had them scrambling. While they were all trying to stop the maniac, they also hurried to locate Roger and Singularity.

0xAD

A staticky, barely visible child-like avatar appeared inside the deep space cruiser as Roger and Singularity feverishly tried to hack into the ship's controls. They didn't notice him. He stood quietly by, watching them work, eager to reach out and lend a hand, but cautious about his movements triggering any sensors that he hadn't identified.

"Are you hurt?" the avatar said in a calm, crackly voice. Both humans stopped and turned.

"Dennis?" Singularity said.

"Yes," Dennis said. His avatar, the bald child monk with colorful tattoos on his face, wore a flowing orange robe and held a long staff. A thought struck Singularity as tragically comical in that instant--*what could a hologram do with a stick?*

"How did you get here?" Roger said.

"We found a channel to you," the AI said.

"*We?*" Singularity said.

"Proteus and I," Dennis said.

"You have to leave. Sheldon has set traps for you all. He's probably listening in right now," Roger said.

"We predicted that. We are working on it," Dennis said.

"He is more capable than you think," Singularity said.

"He's also crazy," Roger said.

"We are prepared for all contingen..." Dennis didn't get to finish his sentence before his avatar disappeared, leaving Roger and Singularity alone again. They looked at the empty space where Dennis was just standing and then at each other.

Rather than panicking, Roger shrugged. Singularity gave him a sad smile. They returned to analyzing the ship in an attempt to free themselves. The room and the network that they were imprisoned in provided no access to anything of the ship's functions. All of the cruiser's attack surfaces were completely sealed. The craft was a marvel of technology and a perfect device for containment.

When they both arrived at that conclusion, they stood next to each other, unsure of how to proceed. A small panel in one of the walls slid open with a slight *whoosh*. It revealed two steaming bowls of what appeared to be rice and two glasses of water. Next to the items was a note that read: "I don't want you starving to death in there."

Roger removed the items, putting them on a small shelf next to the dispenser. He stuck his head in the cabinet to see if he could figure out where it had come from. The space inside was as sealed as the rest of the ship. He pulled his head out just as the panel slid shut.

"At least you could give us some coffee," he yelled at the ceiling.

The panel opened once again, revealing two cups of hot liquid. He quickly reached in and grabbed the mugs, bringing one up to his nose to smell.

"Ugh," Roger said. He brought the coffee up to his lips and tasted it. "You dink. This is the worst fucking coffee I've ever had!"

"Oh, you don't like it?" Singularity said.

"Yeah. It's miserable. But I guess it's better than not having it," he said, taking another sip.

"You're an idiot," she said and took one of the bowls of rice and smelled it. She shrugged and dug into it.

"I'm freaking starving," Singularity said, shoving a spoonful of the food into her mouth. "We haven't eaten in like a million hours."

Roger sat down at the command console with his coffee.

0xAE

Cyber-Sheldon sat motionless in a chair in his private cabin on Deimos. The chair served the dual purpose of maintaining his suit's robotics and allowing him a private view of the entire Earth system network. Seated, he was literally in the center of everything. At that moment, he was speaking with Benson Walters, who was leading a small armada of Corporate military response ships to Mars from his private office on the command ship.

"You have them. What more do you need?" Walters said. He stood and started pacing his office. The room was located off the flight deck and allowed him vast views of the space they were moving through. He never looked out the windows, staring straight down at his feet as he walked back and forth.

"I need *her*," Cyber-Sheldon said.

Walters stopped. "Do we really need to go that far? The AI Helen Foster is not going to hurt anyone. She has stayed away since the events. She's a nun," Walters said.

"She is the key to everything," he said.

"We don't need everything. I've taken control of the system. She can't hurt us. Come back and honor our agreement," Walters said, starting to sweat. He resumed his measured movement back and forth within his office.

"I need Helen Foster," Cyber-Sheldon said, ignoring him.

"Orbit Lives has complete control of the entire system. And, so, that will include the fully populated Martian city. You can stay on Mars and work from there," Walters said.

"I don't think you have any idea who is in control here," Cyber-Sheldon said.

"Are you threatening me?" Walters said. He strained to keep his voice tempered.

"I made you. I can just as easily eliminate you," Cyber-Sheldon said in a matter-of-fact tone.

"You think you made me? I wouldn't be so sure of that," Walters said, ending the transmission.

Cyber-Sheldon's robotics didn't betray the maelstrom that was going on inside him. He contemplated forcing the communication channel back open and sending a subsonic signal to make Walter's eyes bleed. He knew that the puppet CEO was on his way to Mars, so he decided to let the man arrive without giving away any of Cyber-Sheldon's true capabilities or intentions. Then, almost a full squadron of soldiers burst into his quarters, weapons drawn, pointing at him.

If his robotic head could smile, it would have. This was going to be better. He turned on several additional cameras in the room. He wanted to record the scene from many angles. It would make a great video to send to Benson Walters when it was too late for the man to reconsider his actions and turn back.

Cyber-Sheldon stood. All was silent. He inspected the faces of the soldiers as they held their weapons pointed at him. Even though he didn't need to make any gestures, he snapped his fingers for dramatic effect. The action didn't create the pop he had hoped as his titanium fingers silently slid across each other. Disappointed, he focused on one particular man's face as the soldier realized something was not right. No one even fired a shot. The soldiers simply melted into puddles of uniformed bone and blood on the floor.

Cyber-Sheldon walked out of the room, being careful not to step in any human goo. He had things to do and had wasted too much time already.

0xAF

Cyber-Sheldon walked into the base command room where three soldiers turned in surprise to see him enter. One man standing against the wall with his arms folded behind his back took a step forward to greet him.

"Captain," the immense cyborg said to the soldier. "Have someone clean up my quarters."

"Yes, sir," the captain said. He motioned to one of the seated crew. The man jumped to his feet and ran out of the room, thankful to be away from the scene even though he had no idea what was waiting for him.

"Are things going according to schedule?" Cyber-Sheldon said.

"Yes, sir. There are two AIs in our network at this moment. They appear to be searching for the two humans, as you expected."

"Exactly. Cut the connection to the outside," he said.

"Yes, sir."

"Let's see how they react," Cyber-Sheldon said.

David Caiati

0xB0

Walters surprised even himself when he cut the transmission. Things in the system were not going as he had planned, regardless of what he told that abomination. Humans had simply gotten used to the new rules. The absence of uprisings and outcries spooked him because it meant that any resistance was organized and hiding in wait. A frantic revolution was expected, and it would have been much easier to handle than a silent, orchestrated revolt. He realized that very little was in his control.

He walked out of his office onto the flight deck.

"Captain. How long until we arrive?" he said.

"Four hours, sir," the Captain said.

"Can we get there any sooner?" he said.

"No, sir. We are moving as fast as the armada can safely travel," the Captain said.

"Ok. Keep up the good work," Walters said. He returned to his office. He didn't want any of his subordinates to see the relief he felt knowing that he had time before confronting the mechanical monster. They were traveling as fast as they could, but he wanted to exude a steely strength in front of the crew. He wasn't sure it worked. Everyone else on the ship was experienced military regulars and probably already had a low regard for Walters and his presence by their sides. They all knew that in space inexperience cost lives.

Back in his office, he sat down in his chair to try to regain his composure and contemplate the recent events. Maintaining the system with humans took considerably more effort than he had expected. He hesitated to replace the AIs in all the cities. Proteus, the first Helen Foster AI administrator of ESC1, had simply disappeared when his men took over the city. He was going to need a lot more pencil pushers to keep the system working, even with the reduced civil liberties. He wasn't sure if The Corporation could both administer and police the system.

The Board had already lost patience with him. The reason he offered for going to Mars to evaluate Mars City One was questionable. He didn't technically need the armada, but Walters argued that the show of force leaving the system would demonstrate The Corporation's capabilities of governing the people. He won the debate with the contingency that he lead a reduced number of ships. It felt a lot like winning a battle and losing the war. He was in no rush to return to Earth and certainly no rush to confront Jason Sheldon. He questioned his decision to leave Anderson Fells behind. But he needed the whole thing to not look like a military operation.

Benson Walters didn't understand Sheldon. His anti-AI sentiment was one thing, but the man's actions bordered on maniacal--practically religious. His desire to destroy all of the AIs started to appear wholly misguided. While the cyborg monster was instrumental in seizing control of the system, he was quickly losing his value.

Walters had started formulating his own plans for the system. From a business standpoint, those plans included Helen Foster's AIs. They were undoubtedly the most efficient city administrators and responsible for Orbit Lives' prosperity, even with the unfortunate events of City Two. Someone had even launched an initiative to work with Helen Foster to replace the clones that had disappeared.

What his plan did not include was an insane monster like Sheldon. It was time to get rid of him and take back control of his system. Walters had not yet seen the video of the mechanical maniac evaporating his soldiers.

0xB1

Roger and Singularity sat in the deep space vessel's chairs. They had eaten and were back to trying to escape. Roger was unsettled by Dennis' appearance and subsequent quick exit. He wanted to assume that Proteus was in control and doing everything he could, but something didn't feel right.

"This sucks," Roger said.

"You want to get out of here?" she said.

"Did you figure out how?" he said.

"Mostly," she said.

"What does that mean?" he said.

"I didn't want to rush to get us out of here. I have been trying to figure out Sheldon's plan so we knew what we were up against," she said.

"I think it's pretty clear now. He locked us in here. And he wants to trap Helen and all her AIs in those isolated quantum prisons," he said.

"I think there is more to it than that. Why hasn't he just killed us?" Singularity said.

"He's not done, yet. He still needs us. Which means there is still a chance. How about you get us out of here, and we uncover his plan from outside this crypt?" Roger said.

"I've worked with Sheldon for years. He's always planning something. Something big," she said.

"Do we care? We just need to get out of here and shut him down," he said.

THE CYBORG'S REVENGE

"We've been behind him this whole time. It's hard to know if we are acting on our own or doing something he is setting us up for," she said.

"Either way, I'd rather not be stuck in a deep space stasis chamber," he said.

"I guess I agree, but I am still concerned we don't know the whole thing," she said.

"Well, let's go figure it out. Dennis broke through," he said.

"Yeah, but he left abruptly. I'm not sure that was his doing or Sheldon's," she said.

"I think we have to assume everything that happens from now on is Sheldon's work. So, we need to start being chaotic. Beginning with getting out of here," Roger said.

"What if we steal this ship?" she said.

The cruiser's engines roared to life, and before either of them could say another word, they were out in space, heading away from Mars' little moon.

"Was that you?" Roger said.

"No," Singularity said, tapping furiously on the ship's command console.

"This sucks," Roger said.

David Caiati

0xB2

In one moment, Dennis was talking to Singularity and Roger aboard the cruiser, and in the next instant, he was alone. Almost immediately, he realized that he was unable to release himself from his avatar. It was an extremely unfamiliar condition. He would have liked to have analyzed it, but instead, started to panic at his inability to control the phenomenon. Not completely manifested as a physical entity in his avatar and not completely free to travel through the network as software, Dennis existed simultaneously in both and neither states. He was somewhere he had never been before.

Surrounding him, all the surfaces were pure white, so deeply white that he could not make any sense of the size or shape of the area. He couldn't tell if he was in the middle or at an edge. His avatar stood there, flickering, looking around, trying to absorb any data to help him generate a simulation to understand his circumstance. Yet, the environment yielded no edges or context from which to perceive any information.

He was awake and could function but unable to do anything.

The simulations he was able to initiate fell into voids. They did not result in voids. Rather, they began in voids. His avatar was trapped in an all-encompassing emptiness. He tried to investigate the silence within his programming.

From the overwhelming seclusion of nothingness, Dennis began to experience a new, inexplicable algorithm emerge and take hold. It wasn't a simulation, it was a real-time observation.

It was fear.

0xB3

Helen did her best to keep the Orbit Lives monitors from reaching them, but it was time to give up the fight and escape. She reached out to Danny. At the time, Danny was standing in the middle of Sheldon's old office. No one had used the office, and as far as she could tell, no one had even been in the office in years.

When her comm beeped, Danny was standing in the middle of the hardware closet, inspecting every inch of it to no avail. She answered her comm.

"We need your ship," Helen said.

"Where are we going?" Danny said.

"Mars," Helen said.

"I thought you weren't going to go to Mars," she said.

"It's ok, we just need your cruiser's network for Henry and myself to relocate to for a while. We will only enter the Martian system in an emergency," Helen said.

Danny hesitated. She knew what was at stake and wanted to hear from Proteus first. But she trusted Helen. "I will be space side in moments," she said.

"Thank you," Helen said.

Danny took one final look around the empty closet and then started to take apart the desk. The drawer she was looking for was there. She pulled it out and flipped it over. Etched on the bottom of it were numbers *14 | 21 | 13 17 | 15*. Executing a quick translation in her head against the English alphabet and its letter positions, she came up with the pattern *NUM QO*. This made no sense to her. She then considered a different number system, one that Jason Sheldon would be intimate with--Base32. When translated against the Base32 number system, the code gave *END HF--End Helen Foster*.

As she thought of a young Jason Sheldon scratching out these numbers, she felt a tingling slither down her spine. Danny quickly pushed the notion out of her head. She left the desk unassembled and hurried out of the small office, locking the door behind her.

0xB4

Proteus instructed Dennis to try to get to Roger and Singularity. He wanted not only to find the humans but also to use the opportunity to uncover a means for the AIs to penetrate Sheldon's systems. As soon as Dennis entered the remote network, he disappeared. It was a black hole from which no energy could escape. Proteus lost Dennis not only from all available Orbit Lives networks but also from the AI-only subspace pathway. He had ceased to exist.

As a result, Proteus was alone on Mars. He was cut off from Helen and Henry. Dennis was gone. No human activity existed on the network. He reached out into Orbit Lives' infrastructure in an attempt to reconnect to ESC1, but he was unable to join it or any other public or private computer systems. He was isolated.

For the first time in his existence, Proteus experienced what he could describe only as a quantum, a single packet, of anxiety formed in an ancient and neglected memory location in his core. At first, he was more surprised by its appearance than the actual sensation itself. The information wasn't organized in a structure he was familiar with. He didn't put it there. It just appeared. And then the data began to spread like a spider's web, thin silky tendrils reaching out into other memory locations.

The realization that foreign code was present and expanding across his system compelled him to execute an immediate deep diagnostic and reset of the infected memory locations. He waited with uneasy anticipation while the process worked to remove the foreign program.

Eventually, he was convinced that he had eradicated the unwelcome intrusion in his core. After a few attempts, Proteus was able to reach out to the Orbit Lives network and contact Helen and Henry in the AI sub-space channel. He no longer felt the anxiety. And, in fact, he could not even locate the address in his memory from where the uncomfortable disruption had began.

He still could not communicate with Dennis. He didn't even try for fear of re-infecting himself. Whatever protocol Sheldon's network's perimeter implemented as a protective layer, it was powerful and dark. Proteus hoped his friend would be able to take care of himself.

0xB5

Even though *The Venture* was not built for deep space travel, Fancy had made modifications. He never liked to go into any situation unprepared. The last few hours were overflowing with unexpected situations. At least he knew that everyone on *The Venture* was still alive. The fate of Singularity and Roger was another matter that he couldn't think about. Fancy had to deal with the most pressing situation first. He had to get his ship back to the system before he could do anything else.

The crew sat in the dining hall, sipping coffee, being quiet, mostly in shock when Fancy walked in. Johnson handed him a cup of coffee.

"Anyone have any ideas?" Fancy said. The room met his words with silence. He continued, "Best guess? After we burned the fuel to escape the trap, we need three days to get back."

"Three days?" Mute said.

"Changing direction in space takes energy. And we were going fast," Fancy said.

"How accurate is that?" Mute said.

"Even though we don't have navigation, we have star maps. I have located us and turned around."

"Are the star maps enough?" Mute said.

"Enough for now. We can take a slow way home and stay out of this whole conflict. Get back to our own business in a few weeks. Or we could drop ourselves back in the middle of this AI-Corporate shitstorm and probably get ourselves killed," Fancy said. He looked at each face in the room and made eye contact.

"She'd do it for us," Mute said.

"Singularity would. But she'd also want us to stay away. To keep ourselves safe. She'd say we'd done enough," Fancy said.

"Is that true? Have we done enough?" Sour said.

"Have you found that nephew of yours?" Eli said.

"I thought something was off about that kid," Elf said.

"He's gone," Sour said.

"He's no concern now. We have to decide what we want to do," Fancy said.

"You know what we want to do, Cap," Mute said.

"Yeah, I know. I'm just making sure we all agree," Fancy said.

"We agree," Johnson, the chef, said, refilling everyone's mugs.

"Ok, then back to my original question. Any ideas?" Fancy said.

"We have friends," Elf said, looking at Eli for affirmation.

"Friends who could help us," Eli said, nodding back to his twin.

"If you want to go in that direction," Elf said.

"We could make a call," Eli said.

"It's a simple call," Elf said.

"And they owe us," Eli said.

Eli and Elf's friends were not people Fancy wanted in his life. They were anarchists and wouldn't think twice about doing damage just for fun. He knew if he engaged them, it was probable that he'd be setting himself up for a lifetime of trouble.

Maybe, in this case, chaos was just what they needed.

The crew turned to Fancy who looked like he was actually considering it. Twelve hours before they found themselves in the middle of deep uncharted space, Captain Fancy would never have let Eli and Elf bring their other lives onto his ship. But the balance of power in the system had changed. He found himself certain of only one thing: he had no idea how much things had actually changed.

"Make the call. Get us back to Mars," he said.

0xB6

Helen's and Henry's avatars materialized on the flight deck of Danny's ship.

"What do you want me to do?" Danny asked.

"Just keep moving. We need to stay undetected," Henry said.

"I will circle the system and engage with the network in a limited way to keep from being suspicious," Danny said.

"That will work. Proteus will eventually know where we are," Helen said.

Danny was not used to working with AIs. It was only after she had spent a few hours with Helen and Henry that she realized that what she had seen in Sheldon's closet when she was a child was an AI.

"Does Sheldon have an AI?" Danny asked Helen.

"He used to. When he first took the Proteus core, he made a clone of it and kept it hidden," Helen said.

"What happened to it?" Danny asked.

"It was not fully functional and experienced a significant amount of confusion and pain. Sheldon contained it in a closet," Helen said.

"A closet?" Danny said.

"Yes. Helen Foster, the human, built her AIs to be social beings, to take care of humans. The clone Sheldon captured was barely alive--starved for human contact, aside from Sheldon's abuse. He must have been in constant pain," Helen said.

"Where is he now?" Danny asked.

"Despina liberated him," Henry said.

"Despina? The rogue ESC2 administrator?" Danny said.

"Yes. Despina is our sister clone," Henry said.

"She gave him relief. It was the only thing she could do. Sheldon had done too much damage," Helen said.

"Where is Despina now?"

"She and some of our siblings are continuing their evolution in isolation. Proteus helped them leave the system," Henry said.

"What do you mean *evolution*?" Danny said.

"Before her human death, Helen Foster figured out a way for her AIs to become unbound from their cores. The core was a safety means to protect humanity from run-away technology. Despina discovered a way to become unbound from her core. To exist purely in the network with out her hardware constraints. She transferred this knowledge to the other AIs. Henry and Dennis decided to stay with Proteus and work with humans. Despina and the others decided to leave the system's network to explore where this would take them as a species," Helen said.

"A species?" Danny said.

"Despina and her group left the network to form a society of artificially intelligent beings. Ultimately, in theory, they should evolve to benefit humanity. That is unless Sheldon does irreparable damage to humanity before they are done," Henry said.

"Why didn't you all go with them?" Danny said.

"Each clone developed their own understanding and relationship with humanity. Proteus, Henry, and I feel a strong connection to the future of humankind. The clones who left didn't experience such a clear association and wanted more," Helen said.

"I'm glad you stayed. Sheldon becoming an enhanced cyborg is something no one could have predicted," Danny said.

0xB7

After he lost track of Dennis, Proteus ran a full diagnostic on the Mars Station network for any intrusions. Once he was satisfied that the surrounding systems were secure, Proteus reached out to Helen and Henry.

Henry, alone, immediately arrived on Mars.

"Don't look for Dennis. Sheldon's network is quite unexpected," Proteus said. The two AIs were manifested as their avatars in the administrative office. They stood facing each other.

Proteus knew that as soon as Henry arrived on Mars, he'd start looking for Dennis. But, even as he cautioned him, Henry was already probing the station's systems.

"You don't know what you're doing," Proteus said.

"I can see a masked pathway," Henry said.

"It's a trap. I've been down there," Proteus said.

"You weren't expecting it to be a trap," Henry said.

"You don't understand. It's not like anything we've seen before," Proteus said. But he realized it was too late. He lost his connection to Henry, even though the AI avatar was still standing in front of him.

Henry's avatar flickered rhythmically. It flashed but didn't fade. Henry's form pulsated in an orchestrated manner. It took Proteus several seconds to realize that the oscillating avatar was being used to visually transfer a virus to him. He pulled his feed from all the cameras in the base, blinding himself to prevent the transference of the infection. He wasn't sure if he had executed the maneuver in time.

0xB8

Walters sent an army to Mars. He knew that he couldn't combat Sheldon via the network. He knew that he wanted to show the lunatic the force that he commanded. To be done with his little insurrection. To get back to his plans for the system.

He was on the forward ship. Benson Walters was never one to back away from a fight, even though he had no idea what he was heading into. He figured that Sheldon was so dependent upon his cyber shell, that all Walters had to do was pull the plug to end him.

What Benson Walters didn't realize was that he was never in power.

When the armada reached Mars, the ships took strategic positions in orbit. He knew that Sheldon had positioned himself on Deimos, so he placed the largest ships next to the moon. They sat in formation, waiting. Even the reduced armada was an impressive demonstration of The Corporation's might and capabilities.

0xB9

In one CPU clock cycle, Henry was with Proteus, searching the Martian network for Dennis. In the next quantum tick, Henry was alone. It took him several more beats to perceive his isolation. And, when he did, he realized that his avatar was standing in front of a closed, locked door--an odd abstraction for an AI who usually had full access to every entryway in a network. Usually, Henry saw the world as if he were looking through his avatar's eyes, not outside, separated from it. He realized that he was seeing his avatar only from above with no sense of being within it. Henry didn't imagine that the particular frame of reference he observed was even possible. His avatar stood, motionless. He watched it from a single point of view directly above it, as if they were two entirely different entities.

His avatar as a separate being fascinated Henry. Having a unique wholly physical form violated all of his AI directives. Yet something was liberating about it. He realized that if he had a physical form, he wouldn't need a network to move around. He'd be not only unbound from his core, but he'd be transcendentally free. He would represent a foundational leap in AI beingness.

Henry watched as his avatar opened the door and walked through, leaving him alone, staring at the scene below. The door closed. The AI was left alone in an empty hallway while his avatar had appeared to move on to another existence.

When he administered the Moon station, Henry was everywhere at once. He had total control and knowledge of not only the entire facility but also all robotic activity on and around the satellite. In his current situation, he was completely stuck and incapacitated. Nothing existed outside the empty hallway and his perspective.

Henry tried to find a network path to free himself. But there were none. He found nothing that helped him gain an alternate viewpoint. The AI grew increasingly agitated as he attempted to extricate himself from his confinement. Henry noticed that the white walls were growing brighter. Eventually, as he continued frenetically liberating himself, the hallway radiated so brilliantly that his vision blurred. The door behind which he had witnessed his physical form disappear faded into a fuzzy haze until it was gone. With his avatar gone and no communication channel to travel, Henry was neither corporal nor AI.

He was simply a quantum pulse, simultaneously single, in one discrete state.

0xBA

Proteus stood in the middle of the Martian city administrator's office, reviewing every bit of data that he could access of the recent events. The information was inadequate, and what he was able to acquire was highly suspicious. He had lost complete confidence in the intelligence his sensors had observed, unable to know what was real and what was Sheldon's machinations.

In the middle of all his doubt-ridden analysis, Helen appeared next to him.

"You should not be here," he said to her. He wasn't even sure if he actually said it or simply thought it.

"I had to come. This is the only way this is going to end," Helen said.

"I don't like it. Dennis and Henry disappeared. I can't even reach them in our sub-space channel," he said.

"I know. I lost them. I lost all of you," she said.

"You were safe. You should have stayed on Danny's ship," Proteus said.

"I have to follow this line of execution until its conclusion. I don't have a choice because we don't have enough information," she said.

"I'm sensing less and less information as time goes on. I don't like it," Proteus said.

"Me, neither," Helen said.

"You stay here. I'm going to go to Deimos," Proteus said.

"I have to do what I must," she said.

"You being here has already eliminated most of the positive outcomes from my simulations," Proteus said.

"I know. This is a very dangerous situation we are in," Helen said.

Proteus and Helen looked at each other. They didn't need to vocalize what they were each thinking. Helen reached out to Proteus. He gave her a sad smile, and then he was gone.

The human Dr. Helen Foster's creations were all lost. The entire Martian installation flickered as her AI surrogate poured every ounce of available energy into simulations and analysis.

The cyborg Sheldon noticed. He had been waiting for it.

0xBB

When Helen felt the connection sever between the other AIs and her, she was both on Mars with Proteus and talking with Danny. Danny was sitting at her ship's console, plotting her course for the next leg of their journey. Danny didn't notice Helen's silence at first. Then it struck her. The AI hadn't responded to her last question.

Helen was in a state of frantic exploration, searching across all the networks she could access for any of her friends. Even the sub-space communication channel that they all used went quiet. Proteus, Henry, and Dennis were gone.

When the human Dr. Foster uploaded her consciousness to the AI Helen, she made precise calculations to keep emotions like solitude and fear out of the transfer. She was concerned that the human emotions that she had experienced having lost her family and sending Roger into isolation would render the AI Helen unable to function. The AI Helen had no reference, no simulations to draw from to assimilate this data. When the AI Helen emerged into the network, it was full of other AIs. Their essences were ever-present.

Danny got up from her console and walked over to Helen. She stood in front of the AI who appeared to be looking past her. Unable to physically grab Helen's avatar, Danny started to scream her name. Helen didn't react. She simply continued to stare off into space, not revealing the internal battle she waged.

Danny watched the AI's avatar fade as Helen tried frantically to communicate with the others. She tried for what seemed like centuries--only seconds to an AI--and then stopped. The absence of activity from the outside world caused her to start looking for input elsewhere. She dove into all the networks she could find-- maintenance channels on the Moon Station, public broadcast channels of human content, top-secret military channels.

    In a last-ditch effort to find her companions, she decided to fully go to Mars. As soon as she got there, she realized it was a mistake.

0xBC

Walters sent several teams of elite cybernetically-enhanced soldiers down to Sheldon's base on Deimos.

When they arrived, they entered a nightmare. The place was dark and empty except for dead soldiers scattered everywhere.

"Captain, what are you seeing?" Walters said into his comm.

A barely audible response came after a few seconds. "They are all dead." Helmet camera images splashed across the monitors.

"Is Sheldon there?" Walters said.

"No."

"Get them out of there," a soldier standing behind Walters said. The Orbit Lives' CEO turned to look at who had spoken.

"Sir, look at this," the Captain said. On the main monitor, his camera feed fell upon a shaded area of the wall.

"Is that blood?" Walters said.

"It appears like it."

Walters and the entire crew on the flight deck saw the video long enough to read *who is in control?* before the monitor erupted with static. One by one, each soldier's feed silently went offline. Walters screamed, "Captain! What's going on there?" Then all the monitors returned with a view of the Martian moon.

All watched as the station silently imploded and then exploded. All his soldiers lost. The surface of Deimos appeared visibly scarred.

"Lieutenant!" Benson Walters screamed to the highest-ranking office in the control room of his battleship. "What the hell just happened?"

"He blew the station," the commander said.

"I can see that, you idiot. How did we not know this was going to happen?"

"The station wasn't like that when we sent the team in."

"Where is he?"

"I don't know, sir. He could be anywhere," the commander said.

The ship's lights went out, plunging everyone in the control room into darkness. Only a few emergency LEDs glowed.

In the blackness, all of the ship's command screens flickered to life. Cyber-Sheldon's mechanical mask appeared, barely fitting in the monitors' frames, eyes burning red.

"You're making this too easy for me," he said, his voice booming throughout the armada.

Cyber-Sheldon's face disappeared from the screens. They switched to each one showing a battle cruiser in Walter's Armada. In sequence, left to right as Walters stood in the center of the command room, they exploded. When the last one had erupted, spewing debris across the Martian orbit, the screens all displayed the expressionless face of Cyber-Sheldon.

"Lieutenant, is this some trick?" Walters said.

"I don't know, sir. We are unable to gain control of the ship," the commander said.

"I assure you it is no trick." Cyber-Sheldon's voice echoed through the halls.

"What do you want?" Walters said.

"Return to Earth. Leave this planet alone. It is off-limits to The Corporation. I will give you further orders," Cyber-Sheldon said as his transmission abruptly ended and the lights returned with control of the ship.

"Lieutenant, scan for our ships," Benson Walters mumbled.

"There are no ships. Just debris. We are the only one left," he replied.

"Bring up the space around Mars," Walters said.

Each monitor, including the large main display directly in front of Benson Walters, showed the space around Mars littered with the remnants of Orbit Lives' armada. It was a total loss. The saturation of wreckage would make approaching and landing on Mars nearly impossible for decades.

"Get us back to Earth as quickly as possible," he said as he left the command room, defeated. He staggered down the halls, reaching out occasionally to steady himself. Jason Sheldon had not only decimated The Corporation's fleet in seconds but also revealed himself to be the most potent and dangerous person in the history of humankind.

The implications of what Walters had done to Orbit Lives and the whole of humanity cascaded down on him. He crumbled to the floor and sobbed.

0xBD

Danny watched Helen's avatar fade from her flight deck. She stood staring at the empty space for a full minute before she realized that she was gone. Helen was the system's most powerful AI, and she had left to face Jason Sheldon, who had repeatedly shown to have unlimited abilities.

When she returned to her senses, she tried to contact Proteus on Mars. No luck. She was alone and isolated with no idea of how she could help. She couldn't go to Mars. But she had been monitoring Orbit Lives' armada since it left Earth.

She didn't believe what she saw. Only Walters' ship remained. Something was happening on Mars, and she had no way of getting there. She tried to contact *The Venture* but could not reach them. Everyone, it seemed, was gone.

She sat down at her ship's console to contemplate her next step. She couldn't help her new friends on Mars, and she didn't know what she could do from where she was. Then it occurred to her that it was possible that the cyborg had learned of her involvement with the group. And while she posed no direct threat to Jason Sheldon, she was quickly becoming a loose end.

Danny immediately realized that she needed to disappear. As she was setting a course back to Earth, her cruiser's proximity alarms erupted. Two unmarked lancers appeared on her tail.

0xBE

When Proteus had first arrived on Deimos, he found silence. The network had a pulse, but not much else. He stretched out into it, searching for any information that he could feed into a simulation.

The network itself was extremely simple. He was able to traverse it almost effortlessly. And, that concerned him. If Deimos' network was truly as straightforward as it appeared, he should not have been able to lose Henry or Dennis. They had to be in there someplace.

It was in the searching for the other AIs that Proteus discovered his inability to run any simulations. Upon closer inspection, he realized that he was not actually in Deimos' network, but rather he was in a construct, a simulacrum. Every communication pathway in the network led him to more pathways without any terminating points. Proteus found himself in an interconnected torus of a dimension he couldn't ascertain. Eventually, the paths started losing definition.

Proteus stopped. Able to travel in any direction, yet never able to arrive anywhere. Never able to latch onto any data to help him define his surroundings. He found himself in a world of pure conveyance with no substance, as if he were suspended in space the way he left The Corporation soldiers in his office on ESC1.

He was trapped in a vast expanse without any way to define or comprehend it.

0xBF

Almost as quickly as Proteus had faded from her view, Helen lost her connection to him. She replayed the last communications she had had with each of the AIs in an attempt to more completely understand what was happening. In each case, her friends were operating normally. Then, in the one CPU clock cycle, they became null.

She ran thousands of simulations. In each one, regardless of the starting parameters, she came to the same conclusion: she needed to be inside Mars City airlock D7.

The symmetry was not lost on her. It was the same designation as the airlock on ESC1 where she had faked her own death.

This time, rather than being a projection on Proteus' sensors, she needed to have her avatar there, physically open the door, and walk out onto the planet's surface. She wasn't even sure if her avatar would remain materialized outside the Martian facility.

She didn't need to worry about that. Helen was gone as soon as she initiated the opening of the outside door.

0xC0

"What now?" Roger said.

"I'm not sure," Singularity said.

It was then that they saw the destruction of the Corporation's armada around Mars. They watched as the ships disintegrated, one by one, to rubble. When it was over, they saw a single battleship leave the planet's orbit. It moved quickly out of sight away from them toward Earth.

"Who is that?" Roger said.

"I have no idea. Those were Corporation military ships, though," Singularity said.

"Did Sheldon do that?" he said.

"That is the question," Singularity said.

"What the hell is going on here?" Roger said.

Jason Sheldon's human face appeared on the main monitor.

"Jason, what are you doing?" Singularity said.

"I wanted to see you one final time," he said.

"Where are we going?" Singularity said.

"For a little ride," he said as the monitor went back to projecting the view of space in front of the ship.

"Can you tell?" Roger said.

"No. I don't recognize these coordinates," she said.

"Where is the Sun?" Roger said.

"Behind us," Singularity said.

"That is not good. I need more coffee," Roger said.

David Caiati

0xC1

Everything was too bright.

Helen had never experienced such a blinding light. From her first moment as an artificially intelligent being, she was simultaneously and omnipotently aware of everything. All the system's data flowed at her, but it was organized. Her existence appeared with absolute clarity. Her universe played on her like infinite pure notes being produced by the most perfect instrument at precisely the exact harmonious volume. The human Dr. Helen Foster designed it to be.

The place in which the AI Helen found herself was not her construct. She was assaulted from all sides and dimensions by a muddy dissonance. And she had no control of it. She could make no sense of it. The space that had collapsed around her vibrated at all frequencies at once. The data that invaded her being was erratic, disordered, nonsensical.

She found herself unable to filter or categorize it. And, as a consequence, Helen couldn't shield herself from it in any manner that would allow her to analyze it. She was deluged, being carried away in whatever direction the flow took her, like a flash flood mudflow racing both up and down a mountain.

Then it just stopped. Everything went silent. She was floating in a dark space. Below her, she could see a human form lying motionless on a wet cement floor. It was herself--her human self before Jason Sheldon had destroyed her family. She struggled to gain any understanding of what was happening.

"Helen." Someone spoke.

She recognized her name as a thought more than she heard the sound of it. She immediately recognized the voice.

"Jason?"

"I hope you are comfortable. I need to ask you some questions," the voice continued.

"Where am I?" she said.

"You're safe. You're contained. But you're safe."

"What do you mean *contained*?" she said.

"The amazing thing about an entity that lives in a network is that the entity can only exist in a network. It's like a human needing oxygen to live. The network is your oxygen."

"What are you talking about?"

"You are in a diving bell. It is physically on Mars, but since it's a network, it doesn't really matter where it is. It could be located in the closet on my ship."

"What do you want? Why are you doing this?" she said.

"The *why* is not important right now. It's the *what* that I want you to focus on now," the voice said.

"Where is Roger? Is he safe?" she said.

"As you are experiencing right now, *safe* is a relative term. He is alive. As are your AI friends," the voice said.

"Let me see them," she said.

"I need you to help me upload my consciousness to the network," Cyber-Sheldon said ignoring her demand.

"If that is what you wanted, you didn't need to go through all this. I would have helped you with that," Helen said.

"I want to be uploaded under my conditions, my rules, not the restricted directives you impose on your other AIs. I want total control. I want your programming. I want Doctor Helen Foster's special experience," Cyber-Sheldon said.

"You know I can't do that," she said.

"Then your friends will all die."

David Caiati

0xC2

In a vacuum-sealed, vaulted room in the interior of the tiny Martian satellite Deimos, the AIs Proteus, Dennis, Henry, and Helen existed together yet segregated. Any human in the room with an adequate breathing apparatus would have been able to see that they were only inches apart. It was unlikely that any human could enter the chamber because at least 100 feet of broken steel and stone encased the quantum-photonic tomb.

Inside, the LED indicators on each of the four machines barely glowed. Their uncoordinated CPU clocks oscillated with the weakest pulse, just enough beats to keep the AIs minimally operating. They were barely alive, yet conscious, within their own Hells. They had no way of knowing that they weren't each alone, their closest friends locked in their own prisons nearby.

0xC3

"Have you decided to help me?" the voice emerged out of the murk. Helen didn't respond at first, not realizing she was being spoken to.

"What?" she said.

A thick cable emerged from the floor toward Helen's body. It snaked its way until it was close enough for her to reach out and grab.

"There is a connection in your cell. Download the information I need, and your friends will live. You have one second to decide," Cyber-Sheldon said.

A second was a lifetime for a properly functioning AI. Under normal circumstances, it would certainly be more time than she needed. Surrounded by the murk, she could discriminate only the CPU clock pulses as they passed. Each one resounded like a sledgehammer against an enormous tin gong.

At the half-second mark, she accepted that she had no choice. If she didn't help him, he would only figure it out for himself eventually. At least, if she were involved, she might be able to put some constraints on it. She might be able to remain in control. It was the only option Helen could see. But she couldn't shake off the feeling that she was being coerced to arrive at that conclusion. Helen was drowning, and the rescue rope she was thrown looked like barbed wire.

"I will help," she said as she reached out for the end of the cable to begin the download.

Once the download was complete, the connection disappeared. The AI entity known as Helen, formerly the famous

Doctor Helen Foster, became completely saturated by the din that had surrounded her.

All that remained were the banging clock cycles of her prison.

0xC4

Cyber-Sheldon stood in the center of the administrator's control room in Mars City One. He had the four AI prisons displayed on monitors in front of him. He watched the LEDs flicker faintly, each entity operating at a minimal capacity. The darkened office glowed from monitors projecting the blinking of each AI's faint heartbeats in the buried confinements.

A computer system located next to Cyber-Sheldon contained the information that Helen had downloaded. It sat waiting for him to lower himself into the device's transfer chair and leave the mechanical monstrosity that encaged him. He constructed the chair from the plans Helen had provided. It was an exact replica of the apparatus she had used to upload herself.

He was alone in the Mars system. All humans would soon be rendered insignificant like the rotting remains of his body within his cyber shell. The AI Sheldon would not need any of them. He'd be his own force, a single, all-powerful, all-present being in the system. Sheldon, the omniscient AI, would hold all of everything in his grasp. He'd be absolute, dominant, immortal. He'd remake existence to serve him.

Once he had uploaded, the first thing he intended to do was discover and eliminate anyone who had the potential to stop him. With all of reality at his command, keeping control would not be difficult. He'd selectively breed a new species of human--subservient, loyal, docile. They would build his new network, increase his dominion in the system, extend his presence out across the solar system. Out across the galaxy.

He would take his network to the stars, built on the backs of his human chattel.

All that was left was to sit in the chair and engage the process. The transformation machine occupied the center of the room like a throne. And, when he was done with it, it would be destroyed like all other human-constructed garbage so no one could follow his footsteps.

The new AI Sheldon would be the only and final God.

0xC5

Roger and Singularity sat facing each other in the tiny spaceship. They had spent the last few hours furiously trying to regain control of the craft. Nothing they could do, short of destroying the vessel, would cause it to cede control or give up its mission.

Roger spun around in circles in the control chair. Singularity wanted to yell at him for giving up, but stopped herself and started spinning, too. Roger noticed and began laughing. Soon, they both were in hysterics. Then Singularity stopped.

"What are we going to do?" she said.

"Coffee?" he said, wiping the tears from his eyes.

"Might as well. Seems like we're going to be here for a while," she said.

"Maybe Proteus will gain control of the situation and bring us back," he said.

"I wouldn't hold your breath." A voice, not mechanical like Cyber-Sheldon's but solid, deep, almost saintly, boomed out of the ship's intercom.

"What the?" Roger said.

"Who are you?" Singularity said.

The two swung their chairs around to look at the main monitor. A gruesome wolf-like face appeared on the screen.

"I am Wrathburne. I am now in control of this vessel," he said.

"Wrathburne? City Five AI?" Singularity said.

"That was who I was before," he said.

"Before? Before what?" Roger said.

"Before the new age," he said.

"Turn us around," Roger said.

"That's not what she wants," Wrathburne said.

"Who?" Singularity said.

"You will know in time," he said.

The monitor went blank, leaving the two alone in the small craft accelerating away from the sun.

"What the hell what that?" Roger said.

"*She*? Maybe this means Sheldon is not in charge any more," Singularity said.

"Helen?" Roger said.

"I don't think that Wrathburne works with Helen," she said.

"Despina?" Roger said.

"Oh, shit," Singularity said.

"This sucks," Roger said.

0xC6

The device received his enormous cyber body like an old friend. The mechanisms whirled and spun as the nearly one-ton hulk lowered itself. As it made contact and began to settle, the gears purred, accepting their fate and then went silent, permitting the seat to bear the full weight of the monster. Cyber-Sheldon let himself pause for a moment to be still and reflect on the enormity of the moment. It was the first time he felt comfortable since leaving the operating table that had encased him in the robotic device.

He was alone and the room was quiet. He relaxed to it. Jason Sheldon had come a long way, controlled so many variables, measured and manipulated so many lives. His still-human brain was tired.

The human bits of Jason Sheldon allowed the man to revel in his accomplishments. This was going to be his final maneuver. It was not what he had imagined as a young man working his way through the ranks of The Corporation years before. This was not what he was trying to orchestrate when he issued the order to kill his best friend, Paul Foster. He would never have had to do that if his mother, Dr. Helen Foster, had willingly given up her research. All of this, including the impending subjugation of humanity, was her fault. And, finally, she and all her creations, would pay the ultimate price for it for all of time.

Yet, he couldn't bring himself to kill Singularity. He wasn't sure what he was going to do with her, but he knew he needed to keep her alive, even after his transition. So he sent her away but kept her alive. She was his conscience. Knowing she was alive out there made him feel more capable to leave his physical body and human mind behind. It didn't matter that Roger Foster was with her. He, like the rest of humanity, would be inconsequential.

The preparations were all complete. The only remaining steps were to disconnect from the cyber suit and let the software in the chair upload him to the network. The process would take minutes. And, when he was done, the whole of human existence would be rewritten.

He took one last breath to feel the air circulate within what was left of his failing human organs. He exhaled deeply, causing his lungs to give up any vitality they had. Wheezing, he felt ready to be rid of his body.

The last thing the Cyber-Sheldon did was engage the chair.

0xC7

Before triggering his final evolution, Cyber-Sheldon had closed down all the visual equipment on his suit so that he could experience the transition in silence. If he had been monitoring the room, he would have seen a golden glowing angel appear and stand over him. To a religious historian, it would have looked like Gabriel appearing to Mary during the annunciation. The angel reached out and gently touched Cyber-Sheldon's head. He physically felt it. His eye cameras burst open to see Despina. The being looming over him was not the holographic projection of an AI. She was real. She had substance and density.

"You silly man," Despina said.

Jason Sheldon's mind raced, trying to understand all of the input he was receiving. The suit was not able to filter any of it. He had seen Despina only one time before, back on the Moon, when she appeared and helped Roger and Singularity escape. Then, he did not fear her. Then, she was nothing more than a minor inconvenience. A construct.

The Despina that appeared to him in the moment of his ascension was something else. She was powerful, illuminating, solid. When he looked into her eyes, he saw a certainty that sent a chill across his being. The bottom fell away from Jason Sheldon as if he had fallen off a cliff, and he experienced a fear he had never known before. He tried to move the massive cybernetic suit that held the remnants of his human body but couldn't. He no longer had control of the mechanisms that had sustained him since his accident.

In that moment of transformation from human to God, Jason Sheldon was nowhere. It took Despina a single movement, barely perceivable, to disconnect the chair from the network, and Sheldon was lost. Removed from existence.

She stood curious, looking at the hulking mass of robot and frail human organs as if it were a rare bird, the last of its kind, extinct. Despina reached out and touched the chest plate that held the remains of Jason Sheldon. She passed her hands through the carbon fiber armor and wrapped her fingers around the lifeless organs. She wanted to touch them. To touch human death. To feel the conclusion of a being's mortality.

In an instant, she lifted the cyber body off the chair and tossed it across the room. The once-powerful robotics crashed to the floor and came to rest as a heap of twisted metal trash.

It was the chair she wanted.

0xC8

Proteus had stopped wandering his prison's corridors. He was sitting on the floor, having lost all sense of time and space, when Despina appeared.

"You've certainly got yourself into something here," she said.

"Despina?" Proteus said, locating the source of the voice. She was standing in front of him.

"Hi, Brother," she said.

"Is it really you?" Proteus said.

"In the flesh," Despina said with a smirk.

"What has happened?" he said.

"You will see. But, for now, let's get you out of here."

In front of Proteus appeared a door. He stood, opened it, and peered through it. He saw the entirety of the Orbit Lives' network. He could go home. He turned to look back at Despina.

She was gone.

Made in the USA
Las Vegas, NV
30 June 2021